THE BAR CODE PROPHECY

THE BAR CODE PROPHECY

SUZANNE WEYN

SCHOLASTIC PRESS
NEW YORK

ISBN 978-0-545-51242-8

10 9 8 7 6 5 4 3 2 1   12 13 14 15 16

Printed in the U.S.A.   23
This edition first printing, September 2012

The text type was set in Sabon
Book design by Christopher Stengel

For my editor, David Levithan, who believed in the first Bar Code book, *The Bar Code Tattoo*, when no one else "got it." With love and gratitude.

■ ■ ■

The author also wishes to thank playwright and friend Edward J. Schneider, who contributed his intriguing ideas to all three Bar Code books. And many thanks also to William Gonzalez for talking this plot through with me at the very start and contributing so much.

PART ONE

"Now is the hour. The time of the lone wolf is over . . . we are all about to go on a journey. We are the one we have been waiting for."

— *Thomas Banyacya*
Hopi Chieftain

ONE

Grace pulled her plastic junior e-card from the front pocket of her metallic silver shorts and handed it to Eric, who was working behind the desk at the rock climbing center. She had been in love with him from afar for years, and now she was up close. Very close.

"In two days I won't have to carry that card anymore," she told him, trying to keep her tone casual. "I turn seventeen on Sunday."

"Happy Birthday," he said, his dark eyes flashing merrily.

This was more than she'd ever gotten from him at school. It was a huge school — a factory for making students, really — and they didn't have any of the same classes or friends. She noticed him in the halls, though. She always noticed him in the halls. Even as she felt herself blending into the crowd.

Eric never blended in. Everyone knew him. He was quite literally a rock star — a rock-climbing star, that was. Olympic team bound. Not like her at all.

Although maybe he *had* noticed her. Because when she'd come here to the indoor rock wall climbing center for the first time, he'd said, "I know you." And each time after that, she'd wanted him to know more.

"Where are you getting your tattoo done?" he asked.

"Since I have a summer job as a receptionist at GlobalHelix, I can get it done on my lunch break," she told him. "But I have to wait until Monday."

She'd never mentioned her job to him before; in the weeks they'd been flirting (well, she at least had been flirting — his intentions were unclear), it hadn't come up. Now, when she mentioned GlobalHelix, the genetics division of the multi-national corporation Global-1, his smile flickered for a second. "After everything that's happened, how is that company still operating?" he wondered out loud. It wasn't antagonistic — he wasn't attacking *her*. But clearly he wasn't a Global-1 fan.

Grace shrugged. "Global-1 has divisions all over the world and one group went rogue with its own agenda. That division has been shut down."

Eric shook his head. "I can't believe they got away with saying that. They had to have known what was going on. Isn't working there kind of banged out? The building is even evil-looking, like it's some kind of a fortress."

An uneasiness filled Grace. Global-1 had always been good to her family and, she honestly believed, good to the world. It took a hit with the bar code scandal, yes . . . but blaming the whole company for that was kind of like blaming a country for what one outlaw town did.

An image of the company's huge, impersonal lobby, with its five-story glass-and-steel ceiling, flashed into Grace's mind. She could see how it would seem like a fortress to an outsider. But she'd been going there her whole life.

"It's only a summer job," Grace explained, instinctively knowing she wasn't going to convince Eric of what the company was about. It didn't seem worth arguing over, not right now. "My dad works in maintenance there. He got the spot for me. A job is a job. You know how impossible they are to get."

"Tell me about it," Eric agreed with a sigh. "I was lucky to get this one."

Grace laughed. "It helps that you're a pre-Olympic rock climber," she pointed out. Everyone at school knew about that. They gathered at the indoor wall in the gym just to see him free climb with amazing speed and agility. "They're lucky to have you working here."

Eric Chaca could have easily acted like a Jock God, but instead he transformed into Mr. Bashful. "Yeah, whatever," he said, not meeting Grace's eyes.

It made her like him even more.

He changed the subject. "So are you are you up for the tattoo or is it banging you out?" he asked.

Grace wasn't really sure how to answer that. It's not like there was a choice involved. You turned seventeen and got the bar code tattoo. Period.

"It makes life so much easier," she said. Immediately, she saw the questions in his eyes. "I know what you're going to say — but, look, they're okay to get now, right? This second generation of bar codes is just what we thought they were at first: They contain basic info like address, driver's license, bank account, and so forth. No genetic information. No nanobots. That's what they say at Global-1."

Eric sighed. "I wouldn't trust them."

Grace glanced at the tattoo he wore. "I guess you must believe them because you have a 'too."

5

Eric rubbed his tattooed wrist and his expression became uneasy. "Yeah, I know. But that doesn't mean I don't regret it sometimes. You had to have been scared by what happened. The nanobots . . . it was like you were being spied on from within your own body, and if they found something wrong, you were nullified."

"But that's not true anymore."

Eric nodded. "Once the nanobots were deactivated, they were supposed to dissolve in six months. It's been exactly six months since they switched them off so they should be gone. I hope so. It bangs me out to think I had molecule-sized robots running around my bloodstream. Your company could have killed me at any time."

This was another reason Grace liked Eric so much: his honesty. She figured the only way to respond was to be honest in return.

"All that is rumor," she told Eric. "It's too easy to blame everything on Global-1. There were nanobots, yes. I'm not arguing that. But the idea that Global-1 was using them to kill people? That's never been proven."

Immediately, she felt she'd gone too far. But if Eric wasn't going to respect her opinions, why bother?

"Grace," Eric said. There was no criticism, no judgment. Just her name. Him saying her name, as if it was something that mattered to him.

"Eric," she said back.

He looked at her a moment, making a decision. Then he reached under the desk and pulled out a small travel drive.

"A Postman handed me this today," he said.

Grace's first reaction was to ask, "Postmen are still around?" She thought they'd been disbanded after the bar code tattoo scandal had come to light. There was no more need for them.

"You might not see them, but they're still here," Eric replied. He extended the black plastic box to her. "It's a message from Decode. Want to check it out?"

Now it was Eric who was making a bold move but burying it in a casual tone. Even though Decode had helped break the bar code scandal, the group was still a nonentity as far as Global-1 and the government were concerned. Grace knew plenty of kids — mostly outcasts — who treated Decode's leader, Kayla Reed, like their own personal hero, keeping pictures of her hanging on their bedroom walls. Grace had never really understood the appeal. Maybe because her parents would have torn the posters down as soon as they went up, considering it disloyal. But also because, while Grace understood what Decode said it was against, she never really understood what they were *for*. She had no desire for society to fall into chaos, and that's what she feared a rebellion would bring.

Still, Eric was taking a risk handing this Decode message to her, especially after he knew she worked at Global-1. It meant that he trusted her. And that was something.

Grace opened the container and eyed the tiny gold chip inside. "Thanks. Can I get it back to you tomorrow?" she asked.

"Sure. Take your time."

There were no more words to say, so their eyes continued the conversation for a moment longer.

I want you to believe in this, his said.

I want you to believe in me, hers said back.

As soon as Grace was seated on the Bullit-Bus whirring softly toward Global-1 headquarters, she pulled her phone from her titanium mesh tote and took out the small case Eric had given her. Opening it, she wet her finger and lifted the chip, sliding it onto the phone's screen. Immediately an image opened.

A handsome young man of about eighteen with wild black curls, cocoa-colored skin, and dancing amber eyes smiled softly at Grace. She recognized him immediately. His face and those of his fellow bar code tattoo resisters had been all over the news for the last six months. He was Kayla Reed's boyfriend and fellow activist, Mfumbe Taylor.

"Mfumbe Taylor here with the latest video update from Decode," the young man on the small screen spoke in a confident, friendly tone. "Global-1 will not let us post our message in public, since they control all means of discourse, but we will still get the word out. We've accomplished so much this past year that it's hard to know where to begin. Since last May, when a bill was passed making it mandatory for all U.S. citizens aged seventeen and above to be tattooed in a visible spot with their own individual bar code, our organization, Decode, has protested and run interference against this unjust law. From the start, we viewed the bar code tattoo as an unconstitutional assault on human dignity and privacy. The reality has proven to be much, much worse."

Grace paused the video to look out the window. The Bullit-Bus was entering the freeway toward Los Angeles. It wasn't long before she'd arrive at GlobalHelix.

Moving her fingers quickly over the screen, Grace fast-forwarded the video. She was pretty sure she knew what Mfumbe Taylor would be saying about the history of the bar code tattoo. The "much, much worse" things they'd found out were now common knowledge. First, they'd discovered that an individual's genetic code was stored inside the bars of the tattoo. People were hired or fired based on what genetics revealed of a person's family health history. Insurance companies didn't want to insure people who had high risks of certain diseases based on their genes. People who were poor health risks couldn't even get loans or be admitted into colleges. Society was being turned upside down based on DNA. Your genes were your fate — and the last word on whether you would succeed or fail in life was tattooed right on your skin.

And then came the nanobots.

The screen offered a link, and Grace tapped on it. She was curious to see what the Decode angle on it would be.

What Have Nanobots Got to Do with It?

Article by Allyson Minor
Reporting from the California Institute of Technology

Nanobots: molecular-sized robots — invisible machinery that respond to mathematical programming. Self-replicating, they can mimic viruses, manipulate nerves, and apply pressure on various organs — including the brain.

Physicists have known nanomachinery was possible since the 1950s. Nobel Prize–winning physicist Richard Feynman was talking about nanotechnology — the extreme miniaturization of machinery — as far back as 1959. He believed that the friction caused by moving parts would be the biggest obstacle. By the 2010s, nanobots were being used in the human bloodstream to take apart cancer cells within the body.

By the 2020s, nanobots acquired sophistication no one would have dreamed of. Everyone who received the bar code tattoo would soon learn how effective and how deadly nanomachinery could be. But they wouldn't even know that the molecule-sized robots were swimming through their bloodstream. That knowledge would come much later, and for many of them, the information would arrive too late.

In the wrong hands — meaning specifically the power-hungry hands of Global-1 — nanobots could be coded to turn deadly against anyone who had them in their bloodstream.

The California Institute of Technology remains one of the nation's centers for robotic research and development. As a student here, working with the renowned doctor Alfred Gold, I was able to assist Decode members in accessing information that led them to uncover the fact that certain algorithms could be used by Global-1 to cause illness and even death in the people who were injected with these nanobots. And since Global-1 had spent billions to successfully get their agent Loudon Waters into the White House, this amounted to complete government control of U.S. citizens. It was as simple as the entry of a computer algorithm into a specific bar code designation.

In November of 2025, all this was revealed to the public through the hard work and bravery of groups like Decode and its offshoot, the Drakians. With information passed to retired Senator Ambrose Young, Global-1 was forced to shut down their bid for complete government control. Decode and the Drakians are still watching it closely.

You should be watching it closely, too.

Be careful who controls your future.

TWO

The Bullit-Bus glided to a stop right in front of the eight-foot wall surrounding the sprawling GlobalHelix facility. Grace dug for her Global-1 ID badge while exiting the bus. Because she didn't yet have a bar code tattoo, she rested her chin on a metal plate built into the wall while a red laser scanned her eye for an identity check. When it had verified that she was, in fact, Grace Morrow, receptionist, a gap in the wall appeared as a security door slid open to admit her.

Glancing up at the huge metal sculpture on the roof — a twisting ladder representing the shape of human DNA, the double helix — she smiled. Birds were perched on its rungs. It amused her that this imposing structure had become an avian perch.

The building housing GlobalHelix might be as creepy as people claimed, but Grace didn't see that — instead she saw how impressively final-level their technology was. They were always on the cutting edge of innovation. And now they were on their game more strongly than ever. Especially since Decode members had attacked the headquarters — hacking the computers and ramming right through the front wall with a tractor trailer — last October. Within days the wall had been rebuilt and was now fortified to withstand anything. Even bombs.

Grace had a hard time reconciling Decode's idea of attackers, vigilantes, and terrorists with the calm, measured face on the message Eric had given her. But the reality was that Decode wanted to bring this whole place down. And they'd bring her and her father down with it, if they had an opportunity. She had to remember that.

Once the whisper-quiet front doors closed behind her, it was a short walk to Grace's station behind the long, curved, marble front desk. She greeted Terri Lin, the elegant woman she was replacing. "Your father was looking for you," Terri told Grace as she lifted her purse from beneath the desk. "He's working on the tenth subfloor now. At least, he was an hour ago."

"Thanks. I'll buzz him in a minute," Grace said, sliding into the springy titanium desk chair Terri had just evacuated. "Did he say what he wanted?"

Terri shrugged. "Nope."

"Okay."

The sun slanted across the marble floor, filtering in through the large windows at the top of the ceiling. The dimensions of the GlobalHelix building always made Grace feel so tiny. She imagined it was how a mouse or even an ant might feel running along the baseboards of a room. Glancing around the huge lobby of steel and glass, Grace wondered if that was Global-1's goal — to make everyone who entered feel small and unimportant. If it was what they intended, they were excellent at accomplishing it. But it was okay by her. Grace didn't mind being part of something substantial and powerful. In a way, it was even comforting to belong to something larger than herself.

Shivering, Grace pulled her lightweight black cardigan from her tote. The central air was on especially high today.

A tall, silver-haired man with vigorous stride and dignified bearing came through the front door and approached Grace. His blue summer suit was crisp. Dr. Jonathan Harriman was like a celebrity at Global-1. Everyone knew that the distinguished Australian gentleman had invented the first bar code tattoos.

"Hello, Dr. Harriman," Grace greeted as she checked the built-in computer monitor. "There are no messages for you yet today."

Dr. Harriman studied her with his intense ice blue eyes. Grace felt as though he was inspecting her for some sign that she might be deceiving him about something. What it might be, she couldn't imagine. "Thank you, Grace," Dr. Harriman said, walking toward the special executive elevators reserved for the top Global-1 employees.

He knew her name, anyway. That was more than any of the other execs here at Global-1 did.

Once Dr. Harriman had disappeared into the elevator, she glanced at the flexible droid cell phone wrapped around her wrist. Quickly unpeeling it, she flattened it on her desk. Since the bar code tattoo scandal broke, some people acted as though all nanotechnology was sinister, but they didn't stop to realize that nanotech made final-level stuff like these flexifones possible. She tapped in the GlobalHelix number plus the extension for her father's phone.

"Sorry, I can't find your dad," a pleasant female voice said.

"Thanks, Tilly," Grace said, hitting the END button. Of course she knew Tilly was just a robotic voice inserted in her phone's Brilliant chip but they spoke so often that Tilly was a part of her life. Whoever had programmed the Brilliant Bot, as the droid voices were called, had made it incredibly lifelike.

If her father was indeed on the tenth subfloor, the phone signal wouldn't reach him. She'd have to use the internal GlobalHelix phone system. But before she could ask the secretary there to contact him, her father turned the corner from the bank of general employee elevators.

"Dad, I was just trying to get hold of you," Grace told him.

Albert Morrow nodded and squeaked out a tight smile, but something told her he was unhappy. "Mom says you went climbing again this morning," he remarked as he brushed some dirt from the pocket of his gray coverall. Grace barely recognized him in any other clothes, since he'd been working here for as long as she'd been alive.

"I got all the way up the intermediate wall," Grace replied, trying to sound as though she didn't have a good idea where this conversation was headed. "Eric, this guy who works there, says he's never seen anyone advance as fast. He's training for the Olympics in '28."

"That's great, but I thought we said you were going to save all your summer money. You want to go to college, don't you?"

"Climbing doesn't cost that much."

"Grace . . . come on. We've talked about this."

"I know . . . I know," she admitted. Grace's family had been hit hard by the bar code tattoo. Her father had been next in line to head the entire West Coast maintenance division until he was bar coded. Almost instantly afterward, his upward rise was reversed. She'd expected him to be angry about this, but instead he'd resigned himself to it. "Survival of the fittest," he'd told her. "And I like being my own man. I'm not management material. Global-1 knows what it's doing." Rheumatoid arthritis ran in his family line and his bar code showed he had the gene for it. In the wake of the bar code tattoo scandal, the government had ordered all contents of the bar code tattoos to be revealed. But the knowledge that the lines of the bar code tattoo contained each person's unique genetic code didn't restore jobs or reverse any decisions made because of the tattoo.

Not wanting to pick a fight over money with her father, Grace attempted a compromise. "How about if I go climbing less often?"

"How about you don't go at all?" her father countered.

"But I love it and it's the only fun I have. Otherwise I'm here all the time."

"I know — because I'm here all the time, too. Now with Mom sick, it would just really help if you would save your money."

"Just twice a week?" Grace pleaded.

"Once a week," her father said. "Look, Grace, do you want to be on the gymnastics team again this year?"

"Of course I do!" Grace cried. She was team captain this year.

"Well, the bill came yesterday. By the end of August they want the uniform fee and the team travel fee."

"Can you pay it?" Grace asked nervously.

"I was going to ask you to pitch in half from your summer earnings," he replied. "You're not a little kid anymore. It's time you take some responsibility for your own expenses."

Grace hung her head, letting her hair fall like a curtain. How she hated this *you have to be more responsible* lecture. She was hearing it more and more every day.

Grace understood that the family was facing hard times. But she couldn't stand the idea of not being on the gymnastics team — or of giving up rock wall climbing. Once a week would be better than not at all, she supposed.

But it meant she'd only see Eric once a week. Right when something was starting to happen.

"I'll treat you to a rock wall session for your birthday," her father added in a conciliatory tone.

Grace smiled at him. "That would be good. A gift card for some rock climbing would be a nice birthday gift, too."

"We'll see." Grace's father kissed her lightly on the top of her head. "Tell Mom not to count on me for dinner. I'm working a double shift."

"All right," Grace said. Her father headed back toward the elevators, and Grace watched him go. When people talked about how evil everyone at Global-1 was, this was not the man they were picturing. But he was just as loyal as any scientist, any administrator.

Working here was a glimpse of the adult world, and Grace wanted to make the most of it. Remembering her birthday, and the tattoo, she hit a button on the panel in front of her.

"Personnel," a voice spoke out.

Grace leaned toward it. "Hi, this is Grace Morrow at the reception desk. I'm going to be seventeen on Sunday, and I'd like to make an appointment to get a bar code tattoo on Monday when I come back to work. Thanks."

As Grace waited for her appointment to be confirmed, she picked up the newspaper Terri had left behind and began reading the lead story.

Pasadena Sun

Washington, D.C. — July 8, 2026

AMBROSE YOUNG TESTIFIES BEFORE SENATE. CALLS GLOBAL-1 EXECS LIARS!

Recently retired Senator Ambrose Young, longtime head of the Senate Domestic Affairs Committee, appeared on the Senate floor yesterday to call for a second full Senate investigation of the multinational corporation known as Global-1. "The first investigation was not sufficiently thorough," he told the Senate. "Global-1 has whitewashed the affair. Once this blows over, they will resume business as usual. Nothing short of dismantling this treacherous corporation will suffice to safeguard our liberty from these pernicious liars."

Senator Young called for the repeal of The Bar Code Tattoo Bill, claiming that President Waters and Global-1 had grossly misled the Senate and the public. Senator

Young based his accusations on information provided to him anonymously.

"This is just another case of Young's continued slander against our corporation and our nation," Global-1 spokesperson Adam Richard said in a statement. "Freedom of speech allows him to say whatever he wants to say, but nothing he says is grounded in fact."

Although Senator Young would not disclose his sources, Richard's statement noted that the former senator's son, David Young, is the driving force behind the dissident group, Decode, which has fought against the bar code tattoo since its introduction in 2025.

David Young was a junior senator from Massachusetts but resigned his seat in protest when the bill was written into law. A prime mover in last December's protest in Washington, David Young was among those jailed and forcibly bar coded.

Ambrose Young has called for the impeachment of President Waters, claiming the president had full knowledge of the true intent of the Global-1 program. President Waters has categorically denied this charge, claiming that not even Global-1 itself was aware that these things were happening, putting the blame on a single department working without corporate or government authorization. Ambrose Young has called for disciplinary action against those responsible for what he calls "egregious violations of American liberties," but so far Global-1 has refused to reveal the names involved. Lawyers working for Senator Young are preparing the legal paperwork needed to force full disclosure from Global-1. In addition, the Young family has filed a private lawsuit against the Waters administration, claiming that David Young was among those targeted by Global-1 nanobots said to induce depression and thoughts of suicide by overstimulation of the vagus nerve.

David Young has not been seen in public for months. In his testimony, Ambrose Young claimed he didn't know where his son was. "I miss David but I can't blame him for going underground. He has made some powerful enemies," Ambrose Young told the press in a conference after his Senate appearance. "His work as head of Decode is far from over, no matter what Loudon Waters and Global-1 would like us to believe."

The Bar Code Tattoo program was resumed in April of this year. "The bar code tattoo is still the law of the land," President Waters told the House and Senate last week. "And citizens aged seventeen and above who do not get it will be prosecuted. Any new program has its problems at first, but the bar code's initial difficulties have been ironed out — and we thank Senator Young and his son for their efforts in that regard. The bar code tattoo remains our best tool for safeguarding every citizen in this dangerous world we inhabit."

THREE

"Grace?" her mother called from the kitchen when Grace walked into the house that evening.

"Dad's working a double," Grace shouted back, depositing her tote on a chair and fishing her phone from it. Her favorite way to relax before supper was to catch up on the day's events and gossip with her best friend, Emma.

"I know. He phoned. Also, some boy called for you."

"On the house phone?" Grace asked. All her friends called her cell number.

"Yes."

That was strange.

"Who was it?" Grace asked. She wanted it to be Eric. Calling her at home would be another big step.

"I don't remember his name."

"Mom!" Grace wailed, throwing her arms wide in frustration.

Grace's mother appeared in the doorway, seated in the wheelchair she'd been confined to for the last six months. No one could explain the sudden weakness in her legs, no matter how many doctors they consulted.

"Was his name Eric?"

"I'm not sure. Who's Eric?"

"Nobody. Did he say anything else?"

Her mother produced a Post-It note with a number written on it. "He said to call him. *Who is Eric?*"

"Just a guy I know."

Grace dashed up the stairs, needing the privacy of her bedroom. "Out! Out!" she shouted at her twelve-year-old sister, Kim, who was lying on the twin bed next to Grace's, polishing her nails.

"It's just as much my room as yours," Kim protested, continuing to apply the silver color.

Sighing deeply, Grace retreated down the hall to the bathroom, locking the door behind her. She sat on the edge of the tub scrutinizing the phone number. It wasn't a number she knew, which was good; it meant it could still be Eric. But why hadn't he called her cell?

Because he doesn't know my number! she realized. He had obviously looked up her file at the indoor rock climbing center, which listed her home number. Or at least Grace hoped so.

Quickly punching in the phone number, Grace waited only a few seconds before a youthful male voice came on the line, saying, "Speak to me, unknown caller!"

"Eric?" She wasn't sure why she asked, since she recognized his voice.

"Grace!"

"Yes, it's me. I got a message to call you."

"Yeah, great! Sorry to call your house. Now I have your number."

There was an awkward pause but Grace didn't care. Eric Chaca had called her!

"So, anyway, here's the thing," Eric said after a moment. "A bunch of us who work here got permission to have a kind of climbing party down at the center tonight after it closes."

"Sounds fun," Grace remarked, her excitement increasing.

"Do you want to come?"

Grace closed her eyes tight and pumped her fist as she fought not to squeal joyfully out loud. "Is it just for employees?" she asked, hoping her voice didn't reveal that nothing on earth could stop her from going.

"Mostly, but other people are inviting friends, and so I'm inviting you," Eric replied. "Can you make it? We're meeting up at ten tonight. I can come by to pick you up if you like."

"All right. I live at —"

"I've got it," Eric interrupted her. "It's in your file. I'll be there at nine-thirty."

"Great."

Grace clicked off the call and released the suppressed cry of thrilled excitement.

Someone pounded on the bathroom door. "Hey, what are you doing in there? I have to get in," her fifteen-year-old brother, James, demanded. Opening the door, Grace smiled into his freckled face. "What are you so happy about?" he asked.

"I'm just naturally a happy person," Grace replied, sliding past him.

"It's probably some guy," James muttered as he entered the bathroom, shutting the door.

Grace was happy to see that Kim had left the room. She shut the door and quickly slid her droid's screen to FACE-TO-FACE and tapped the photo of her best friend, Emma.

"Hologram or screen?" Tilly's velvety auto-voice inquired.

"Hologram," Grace replied.

"Eric Chaca just asked me out!" Grace said to Emma the moment her friend's slightly too-vivid, mildly transparent image appeared, hovering just above Kim's bed.

"Final level, Grace!" Emma cried, her eyes shining, her short neon green curls bouncing. "He's only the most final-level boy in school!"

"He is, isn't he?!" Grace agreed. "I mean, I just can't believe he called me. Eric Chaca!"

"I know! Eric Chaca! Tell me what he said. Tell me everything!"

After Grace recounted everything that had happened, Emma said, "It's nice of your parents to let you go out so late and with a guy you don't know all that well and that they don't know at all."

"Hmmm," Grace hummed nervously.

"You haven't asked them yet?" Emma guessed.

"Hmmm," Grace repeated as her stomach clenched anxiously.

"You are going to ask for permission, aren't you?" Emma checked, anxiety seeping into her tone.

Was she going to ask? Grace wasn't sure. What if her mother said no? How could she tell Eric no, she wasn't allowed? It would sound so juvenile. He might never call her again.

"Grace?" Emma checked. "Tell me you're not going to sneak out."

"It's not like I'd be doing something bad."

"Yes, you would! You'd be sneaking out of the house in the middle of the night." Emma's voice was now fully alarmed.

"But not to do anything wrong," Grace argued.

"I don't know, Grace. Do you really want to be in huge trouble on your birthday?"

"If I'm careful, I won't be in *any* trouble at all," Grace countered.

"Then you had better be awfully careful or it's going to be one seriously banged-out birthday."

Grace didn't mention the Decode message to Emma. It just wasn't the kind of thing they talked about, so Grace had no idea how she'd react. Rebellion wasn't a part of their lives. They liked living within the lines, doing the things that would make their parents and their teachers happy. This was probably why Emma was so surprised that Grace was sneaking out.

For her part, Grace was surprised, too — at how easy it was to convince herself to do it.

"Hey," Emma said as they were about to end the call. "Did you hear there's a meteor heading toward Earth?"

"I heard about it," Grace answered. "It's going to pass us by. They always pass us by, don't they?"

"That's true," Emma agreed. "If a meteor is going to smash into us, I guess there's no sense worrying about whether or not you get caught going on a secret date."

"Yeah, but it's not going to hit us," Grace reminded her.

"Then maybe you should worry," Emma allowed.

■ ■ ■

Grace's luck was holding. Right after dinner, Kim left for a sleepover at her friend's house. Then, at eight o'clock, Grace claimed to have a headache and said she was going to her room to read. By nine fifteen, her hair and makeup were the way she wanted and she had on her jeans, silver hoop earrings, best sneakers, and her new lightweight T-shirt.

With pillows and clothing under her blankets to make it look like she was in the bed, Grace reached out her window until she was able to get hold of the branch of an oak near her bedroom. Once she had a firm grip, the rest was easy. Grace had climbed this tree all her life.

At a bottom branch, Grace dropped to the ground. Not even daring to breathe, she kept in the shadows as she made her way to the front of the house. The neighborhood was quiet. Every time a car came up the street, Grace pulled back farther into the darkness, afraid it might be her father returning from work.

Maybe she shouldn't be doing this, she considered. Her parents would be so disappointed in her if they discovered what she'd done. She should probably phone Eric and cancel. He'd have to understand.

An old black hybrid sports car pulled in front of the house with its top down. The minute Grace saw Eric in the driver's seat she headed for it, all her reservations forgotten. She returned his smile, thrilled that he seemed delighted to see her.

"Hop in," he said, pushing the passenger door open.

Grace was relieved when they finally turned the corner away from her house. She'd made it without getting caught.

"It's nice of your boss to let you use the climbing center after hours," she told Eric. She couldn't tell whether her heart was beating from the thrill of escape or the excitement of the destination.

"He's a good guy. And he approves of what we're doing," Eric said.

"What do you mean?" Grace asked. "What are you *doing* besides having a party?"

Eric stuck his chip-sized music player into an opening in the dashboard and loud rock music instantly blared, making it impossible to talk further. When they were about five blocks from the climbing center, he switched the music off and parked. "Let's do the rest on foot. It will look suspicious if there are a lot of cars in the parking lot."

"I thought you were allowed to be there," Grace said, suddenly nervous.

She took a long, hard look at Eric. How much did she really know about him? The climbing prowess, of course. She knew his parents were Native American and lived in a development across town. She knew he believed in Decode and didn't like Global-1. Other than that . . . there wasn't much. She was taking the way she felt about him on faith, but she wasn't naïve enough to think this was a safe way to judge a person.

"The owner knows we're there, but the Global-1 cops don't," Eric explained.

This didn't make her feel much better.

"Global-1 cops?" she asked. "Why do you . . . ?" Grace let her voice trail off and hurried to keep up with Eric, who was moving quickly ahead of her.

She didn't want to turn back, but she was much more cautious about going forward. The fact that they were hiding from Global-1 police couldn't mean anything good. If she wound up in trouble with the police her parents would never forgive her. She might lose her job. What would it do to her chances to go to college?

Why had she done this? Maybe she could catch a Bullit-Bus back home.

Sensing this, Eric slowed down and turned to her.

"I see something in you," he told her, not meeting her eyes.

What did he see?

Because of the way he was not looking at her, Grace felt he wasn't being evasive, just bashful again. How odd to think that she, nobody Grace, could make a high school superstar like Eric shy.

"I've seen it in the way you climb," Eric went on. "Nowadays, you can tell the people who have a capacity for truth and the people who don't. You," he said, finally matching her gaze, "have a capacity for truth."

"How can you tell something like that?" Grace asked. She wasn't fishing for a compliment. His words mystified her.

"I don't know." Eric lifted his chin and seemed to be trying to find the words he needed. "I think it's in your eyes. They're clear and direct." He smiled. "Not to mention beautiful."

"Thanks," Grace murmured.

"I see it in the way you climb, too," Eric added. "You're physically strong, and once you see where you need to go you head straight for it. Not everyone is like that. They doubt what their gut is telling them so they fumble and slip, but you trust your inner truth. Inside, you're strong. You have a real center, a core."

"I hope that's all true," Grace said, flattered.

"I know I'm right," Eric said. "You can handle truth."

It shocked Grace that Eric had given her that much thought. If they were at the movies or in the cafeteria, his words would have delighted her beyond measure. But they weren't at a Cineplex or in school. They were standing outside the supposedly closed climbing center in the dark, worrying about Global-1 police seeing them.

What truth was he going to reveal? What was it he was so certain she could handle?

And even if she could handle it, did she want to?

Grace's gut clenched and she had the feeling her life was about to change, and she wasn't sure she wanted it to.

FOUR

They didn't need to break in, or force entry. Eric simply waved his bar code across the scanner, and the door of the rock climbing center breezed open. Grace took some comfort in this — it meant the owner definitely had to be on board, or else Eric wouldn't have stamped his information in the entry data.

The place was dimly lit, but Grace heard the murmur of soft voices, even before she could see any people talking.

As her eyes adjusted to the low light, she became aware that the hum of conversation was coming from people who hung in midair, their backs toward her, facing away. Only a few stood on the ground, holding belay climbing ropes attached to the floating people.

Placing her hand on Eric's arm, Grace looked at him with alarm. What was going on?

Eric smiled at Grace's bewilderment. "They're holographic stealth walls," he explained. "During the day we have them amped up so they're a little transparent but viewable."

Grace knew what he meant. The walls always had a slight wavering quality. Sometimes she felt as though she were climbing up a waterfall.

"The walls are really there of course, otherwise you

couldn't climb. But when they're on the lowest setting, the human eye can't see them at all," Eric continued.

"So these people are climbing, not floating," Grace realized. "But how can they climb without seeing?"

"Practice."

Grace shot him a look of disbelief. "Really?"

"It takes a lot of practice, memorization, and intuition. Want to try?"

"It's so weird. I don't think I could."

"We can start with the intermediate wall you did today. I'll set it so you can see it dimly. Then each time you complete the wall, I'll push it back until the wall disappears completely. I'll spot you on belay."

"All right," Grace agreed, warming to the challenge. She would have thought this impossible to do, but obviously people were doing it.

Grace watched as, from behind the front desk, Eric brought into view a wall that had previously been invisible. Strapping on the climbing harness Eric handed her, she hooked onto the rope. Eric took the other end. "On belay," he said, to let her know he had hold of it.

Grace flashed back to the first time Eric had spotted her. There they were — her on the wall, him on the ground, the rope tight between them. It was such a powerful connection, resting your balance, your height, your *safety* on another person. Not only did he have to keep her from falling, but he had to read every move she made, react effortlessly to her painstaking climb. It felt awkward at first, but after a while, she didn't have to think about it anymore. The faith was there. The trust between them was as solid as the wall, the floor, and the rope.

Now, for a brief moment, she felt him on the other end. The weight of him. The force of him. The certainty that he would be there, no matter what happened, no matter what she needed as she rose.

Having just completed the wall that afternoon, Grace scurried up without too much difficulty and quickly rappelled down.

"Final level!" Eric praised her when she was on the ground again. "If I didn't know better, I would think you've been doing the intermediate for years. You look so confident. I'll make it dimmer now, okay?"

"I'd like to try it once more," Grace requested, just to be sure. "I want to really get it into my memory."

"If you think you really need to," Eric agreed.

When she'd completed the wall a second time, Eric once more suggested making it harder to see. "Think you can handle it?" he challenged playfully, his eyes shining.

"Sure," she said, though she wasn't sure at all.

Eric went to the front desk and Grace kept her eyes on the wall as it slowly faded. Her eyesight was excellent but now she was squinting in her attempt to keep the wall in focus. It wavered in front of her; sometimes she couldn't see parts of it at all.

"Try it now," Eric said, returning to ground her.

With a nervous nod, Grace surveyed the wall and saw a darkened square just above her head and thought she remembered it as a handhold. Reaching, she gripped it. From memory, she lifted her knee and found a protrusion she could stand on. Tensing her abdominal muscles, Grace pulled herself up.

"That's the way," Eric encouraged.

The protrusion she was standing on appeared and disappeared as though waves of invisibility were washing over it.

Above her head, Grace sighted another protrusion, reached for it — and missed! Waving her arms, she fell away from the wall.

"I've got you," Eric reassured her as she swung on the rope, her feet kicking. "Focus on the wall. Find your way back."

Grace's stomach seemed to twist and warm liquid bile rose into her mouth. The freakiness of the wall was throwing off her balance and nauseating her. *Do not puke*, she commanded her body.

To her tremendous relief, her insides settled after a moment.

"Okay up there?" Eric checked.

"Okay," she confirmed.

"Go back and find some more holds," Eric instructed. "Take a second to remember where they were. If you relax your eyes and let your focus go soft, you can see them."

Grace discovered that this was true. If she stopped squinting, a pattern of lights emerged. She quickly realized that the lights were protrusions.

With this new understanding of the wall, she began to climb once more.

"Last level of invisibility?" Eric asked when she had once more rappelled down to the floor.

"Oh . . . I don't know," Grace demurred breathlessly. "I don't think I can."

"I know you can," Eric insisted.

"Why don't *you* do one?" Grace suggested.

"All right."

"I'll work the belay rope," Grace offered.

"Don't need it," Eric replied as he unhooked his carabiner from the rope.

"You're going to free climb?"

With a nod, Eric went behind the counter and brought the wall down so that it was completely impossible to see. Returning, he jumped up and appeared to hang in midair. In a minute he was scrambling up, over, and back down.

Grace was transfixed. Eric on his own was beautiful, certainly. But seeing Eric so much in his element, seeing him so extraordinary at something, was a higher power of beauty.

"Your turn," Eric said as he landed next to Grace.

"That was amazing. I could never do that," Grace said.

"Sure you could," Eric insisted. "Look at all these guys doing it." He spread his arm and Grace was once more aware of all the other climbers who seemed to hang in midair. None of them moved with the same speed, fluidity, or self-confidence as Eric did. They went more slowly and methodically — but they were climbing. "You could be better than any of them," Eric remarked. "You have the stuff to be a world-class climber. Like I said, I've been watching you."

"Better than *you*?" Grace asked with a taunting smile.

"Let's not get crazy," Eric teased back. "You have the talent, for sure — but you also have to have the guts for it."

The thinly veiled dare was all Grace needed to hear. Never in her life had she been able to walk away from a direct challenge. "I'm not free climbing, though," she insisted.

"Not yet," Eric agreed. "Of course not. That would be stupid."

Once they were again connected by belay ropes, Grace was ready to try. "This time allow your mind to be soft," Eric advised. "Don't think, just move. You've done this wall a bunch of times now. Your body remembers the way. Let it take over."

Grace exhaled in a nervous waver. "I'll try."

"Breathe deep before you start," Eric suggested.

Closing her eyelids, Grace inhaled, pulling the air down into her lungs before expelling it with a whoosh. Instantly her shoulders loosened, dropping slightly.

"Don't think about anything but your breath," Eric coached. "Stay still until you're ready."

In Grace's mind she saw a picture of the wall as it had been during the day when it was fully visible; then she pushed the image away and began to climb upward.

Grace admired Eric's profile as they drove through the dark streets on the return trip to Grace's house. There was something strong and peaceful about the lines of his chin and nose. Sensing her gaze on him, Eric turned. "You are really a stellar climber," he complimented her. "Totally astral! I can't believe the way you took that invisible wall — and on your first try, too."

"I almost fell when I got to the top," Grace reminded him.

"*Almost* doesn't count." He glanced at the clock on the dashboard. "Hey! Twelve-o-two. Happy Birthday!"

"Thanks!"

They were almost to her house, and Grace didn't want to have him pull right in front. It would be safer if she cut through the backyard behind and went silently back up the oak tree into her room. "Turn here," she instructed Eric. When he asked where they were going, Grace told him her plan.

"You mean you weren't supposed to come out tonight?" he asked.

"No, I didn't ask," she admitted with a shrug. "I wanted to go. I'm glad I did, too. Climbing that invisible wall was beyond stellar. I wouldn't have missed it for anything."

With a grin, Eric pulled to the sidewalk and cut the engine. "We can do it again soon."

His words pleased her, and Grace silently vowed to become even better at climbing, no matter what. Not to impress him. Not at all. But to be that good at it.

A thoughtful look came into Eric's eyes. Even in the dark, she was so aware of them. "Are you really going to be tattooed on Monday?" he asked.

The tattoo. She'd gone for hours without thinking about it. "Sure," she said. "Why not?"

Eric lightly took hold of her wrist, right at the spot where the tattoo would go. "Don't do it," he said.

Grace stared at him questioningly. "You did it," she pointed out once more.

Eric's eyes moved around her face as if he were taking her measure, trying to decide something about her. Then he looked away. "I told you, I'm not sure it was the right thing to do."

"Why not?"

Eric's changing expression told Grace he was on the verge of telling her something . . . but then decided against it. "No reason. Just a feeling," he said, looking away.

"Tell me," she said, sure he was holding back.

"Delay it awhile," he suggested.

It was not the full answer she'd wanted. "What good would that do?" she asked. "If I get caught without it, I'll be arrested. My family will have to pay my legal fees. They can't afford that. Plus, I don't want to start my adult life with a criminal record."

Something in Eric's eyes closed off. He seemed disappointed by her words, and it hurt her that he thought less of her. But what else did he want her to say? That was how things seemed to her.

"You'd better get home," Eric said. Clearly, he was done with the conversation. "It's getting late."

"Tell me why you think I shouldn't get the tattoo," Grace repeated softly. "Please."

He shook his head. "Not tonight."

"What is it?" Grace pressed. "You said I could handle the truth, but you haven't told me anything." Had he changed his mind about her? It hurt to think that might be so.

"Some truths are better not to know," he said.

"Stop that!" Grace insisted, feeling annoyed. Why had he given her so much talk, flattering her that she was strong and could be trusted only to give up on her now? "Tell me what's going on. If there's something I'm unaware of, then I want to know what is. You, yourself, said I could handle it."

"We can talk more tomorrow, if you like," Eric said, and some light came back into his black eyes, as if the shut door had been cracked open a bit. "Are you doing anything special for your birthday?"

"My mom usually cooks my favorite dinner and makes a cake. I'm hoping for a gift card for some sessions on the wall."

"I know it gets expensive," Eric said. "Listen, I'll go with you to your house to make sure you get in safe."

"Just stand and watch. I only have to cut through that yard."

They got out of the car and entered the moonlit yard, keeping to the darker areas. They stood close, and for a moment Grace thought Eric might kiss her there in the shadows. She hoped he would, but he made no move toward her and she suddenly felt foolish standing there waiting. "Thanks for tonight," she whispered, moving away.

When Grace arrived at the oak by her bedroom window, she waved broadly and Eric gave an answering wave before slipping off into the darkness.

As she began to climb the oak, she reviewed the night. She liked Eric so much and he seemed to like her, too. But there was obviously something he wasn't telling her. It made her uneasy.

What was he hiding?

Pasadena Sun
Washington, D.C. — July 9, 2026

NASA ORDERS EVACUATION OF THE INTERNATIONAL SPACE STATION UNTIL METEOR 1 SAFELY PASSES EARTH

In a press conference today in the White House Rose Garden, President Loudon Waters expressed the opinion that "NASA's panicky evacuation of the International

Space Station (ISS) constitutes an extreme overreaction and a waste of NASA's monetary resources."

NASA insists that although astronomers feel confident that the giant meteor will bypass Earth, systems are in place in the unlikely event that there has been an error in calculating the velocity and/or trajectory of the approaching celestial boulder. The controversial approach of meeting a menacing meteor with nuclear rockets is once more being debated in Congress and the Senate. Although nuclear missiles could be used to explode the meteor before it reaches Earth or knock it off its deadly path, the effects of the resulting radiation raining down on the Earth could be, in itself, catastrophic.

"In the meantime, we feel it prudent to evacuate the space station and go to drone backup technology until the meteor is safely on its way," says a NASA representative.

NEDRA, a private commercial space station owned by Global-1, has no plans to evacuate. NEDRA competes with ISS, offering its scientific findings for sale to individuals or other companies willing to purchase its research.

In an anonymous opinion piece appearing in today's *New York Times*, a contributor widely believed to be former Senator David Young, leader of the bar code resistance group Decode, calls this situation just the latest in Global-1's bids to gain control of outer space and corner the market on space travel. "Their careless disregard for human life is once more their trademark and calling card," Mr. Young wrote. "After all that has happened, why is this amoral corporation still being permitted to operate? If we let them get their foothold in outer space, with their privately held satellites and space stations, there will be no fighting them here on Earth."

China and Russia have followed NASA's lead in bringing their people down from space. They have urged Global-1 to do the same.

FIVE

On Monday, Grace took the GlobalHelix elevator to the fourth-floor personnel office. The moment had arrived. The bar code tattoo was the rite of passage that would mark her as an adult. And what choice did she really have? The life of an outlaw, running and working against the bar code tattoo wasn't for her. It would all be fine.

When Grace got off the elevator, she saw a girl she knew from a lower grade in school who had a job as a data-input assistant for the summer. "Hey," said the girl, whose name Grace couldn't recall. "What brings you up here?"

Grace flashed her wrist. "Getting the 'too."

"Awesome. Happy Birthday!"

"It was yesterday, but thanks."

A rush of anxiety ran through Grace as she sat waiting in the tattoo office. When the nurse appeared, she smiled at Grace as she took a blood sample, working the needle with a skillful, practiced touch. Grace waited while the nurse disappeared into the next room and returned with a black machine about the size of a toaster oven: the laser tattooing machine.

With the nurse's guidance, Grace slid her upturned wrist into the machine. It caused only a slight burning sensation as the blue laser lights etched the first two sections of the bar code tattoo onto the inside of her wrist. Numbers, words, and symbols whirred by on a read-out as the lasers worked.

With an unexpected abruptness, the machine whirred to a halt. Grace looked at the nurse quizzically. "Why are we stopping?" she asked.

The nurse poured the vial of Grace's blood that she'd drawn into a glass compartment built into the machine. "We entered your vital information from a disc that's been compiled on you. Now the machine will analyze your blood to add your genetic information."

"I thought that's illegal now," Grace objected, alarmed.

The nurse smiled confidently. "The system has been refined so that only authorized medical practitioners can access your genetics. Employers and insurance companies can't see it. Having ready access to this information could save your life someday."

"How do I know that's true?" Grace questioned.

The nurse scowled lightly and shook her head, silently scolding Grace for her mistrust. "President Waters signed that bill into law just last week. It's against the law for anyone else to access that information. You don't have to worry."

Grace nodded uncertainly. Was it paranoid not to trust what this woman was telling her? What reason would she have to lie?

Eric's voice came back to her. *Don't do it.*

But then she saw her father's face. He'd worked here all his life. Didn't she owe Global-1 that much trust?

"Which kind of bar code tattoo do you want?" the nurse asked. "You can have the traditional rectangle of bars or the new square ones with the bars inside."

"I don't know," Grace replied. "The new ones are kind of cool looking."

"Not as many places take them yet. They need a special upgraded scanner," the nurse pointed out. "On the other hand, some people like them because they don't look like the old ones. It makes people feel safer."

"But is it really any safer?" Grace asked.

The nurse shook her head and smiled. "They're both perfectly safe now."

Once the blood was in the tattoo machine, the blue laser lights appeared once more. In an instant, the bar code tattoo was emblazoned on Grace's inner wrist. She withdrew her hand, rubbing away the burning sensation. The nurse handed her a cool cloth. "In five minutes you won't even feel it," she promised.

A strange elation mixed with sadness swept over Grace. It was done. There was no turning back from it, no more deciding.

"It's like closing a door on your childhood, isn't it?" the nurse said kindly, reading the anxiety in Grace's expression.

"In a way," Grace admitted.

The nurse got up. She'd had this conversation many times before, no doubt. "You'll get used to it very quickly." She displayed her own bar code tattoo. "Soon you won't remember how you ever lived without it."

As Grace headed toward the elevator, she was so engrossed in her bar code tattoo that she walked right into the tall figure standing in her path. "Dr. Harriman!" she cried when she looked up and saw who it was. "I'm so sorry."

"You've been bar coded," Dr. Harriman observed. Grace was immediately struck by how concerned he looked.

"Yes," she told him. "I'm seventeen now."

His expression twisted into one of self-reproach. "Of course you are. How could I have forgotten?"

What was he talking about? Why should he even know her birth date?

"Dr. Harriman?" Grace asked.

Clutching Grace's wrist, Dr. Harriman examined her bar code tattoo. "Go home, Grace," he ordered. "Right away. Wait for my phone call."

"What's wrong?" He was scaring her. "Isn't the Bar Code all right now?"

"No, it's not all right. Not all right at all!"

This didn't make any sense. Dr. Harriman had invented the bar code tattoo. Grace wanted to turn back to the nurse, to ask if she was imagining things. But Dr. Harriman's grip was too tight, too real. His words were too urgent.

"Tell me why it's not all right," Grace said, pointing to his tattooed wrist. "You have one."

"Mine is deactivated. And I wish to God I'd never begun this cursed thing."

Maybe Eric was getting to her, because the moment Dr. Harriman said this, she expected Global-1 police to come storming in, to pin them both to the ground. She expected the walls to cave in and the ground to shake, because that's what listening to this man felt like.

But none of that happened. It was just two people in the

hallway of a corporation, one of them holding on to the other for dear life.

"What do you mean by that? Please tell me," Grace pleaded.

There's a good man, her father had said when she was a child every time Dr. Harriman had walked by. *Great men aren't always good, but this one is.*

"And now you! This has happened to you," Dr. Harriman muttered. Then he came back into focus — not with any answers, but to repeat his instructions. "Go home," he told her. "Go home as if nothing else in the world matters."

He looked around, to make sure there was nobody else nearby. Then he hurried off, leaving Grace standing alone, bewildered, and frightened.

Grace's natural first instinct was to call her father. Heading to the nearest inter-office image phone, she punched in the numbers for the maintenance department, desperate for him to be there. He would dispel her worries. He always had a good way of calming her.

But all she got was the department secretary, who told her, "Sorry, dear, he wasn't scheduled to work today."

Grace punched her home number into her droid cell. "Face. Screen. I don't care!" she cried when Tilly's voice came on asking for instructions.

"Screen only," Tilly chose.

Grace cried out with exasperation when the home voice mail came on.

Where is everyone?

Grace hurried down to the front desk, where Terri had been covering for her.

"Is it done?" Terri asked, looking up from her magazine.

"I'm so embarrassed," Grace told her, "but getting the tattoo made me a little light-headed. Would you mind staying here? I think I need to go home and lie down."

"No problem," Terri said kindly. "Feel better."

Grace quickly gathered her things, making sure to only take what she'd ordinarily take home for the night. The rest would be left behind.

Why do I feel like I'm never coming back here?

It was such a strange sensation, this instinct. But it felt like certainty.

When I get home, everything will be better, she told herself.

But those words also felt hollow, as if she already knew better.

SIX

The Bullit-Bus left Grace off only a few blocks from her house. At first she hurried toward it, eager to find her parents, but Grace slowed her approach as she neared her home, and a heavy wariness came upon her. Pushing back her hair, she surveyed the scene. The front door was open. So was the garage — and both cars were gone. No one, not even James or Kim, would have left the house wide open like this. It was one thing for them to be gone, but quite another for it to be so recognizable. They wanted her to know: *We're not here.*

But where had they gone? And why had they run off so fast?

Grace was a few houses away, hanging back behind the trees, when she noticed the SUV parked at the curb with G1SP written on it. GLOBAL-1 SECURITY POLICE.

The low flame of fear burning in Grace's gut flared into full-blown panic.

What were G-1 police doing in her house?

They have my family, she thought, and at that moment she was ready to go to them, to turn herself in, in order to get them free.

But then she thought, *No.* Because if the police had taken her family, they would have left the cars.

Her family had gotten away. She had to believe it.

A Global-1 officer stepped onto the front walk wearing the usual uniform: black helmet with a mirrored glass visor, black pants, and black shirt. The slightly padded bulletproof vest he wore bore the taser, laser guns, and ammunition of his profession. Turning his head slowly, he surveyed the neighborhood, his handheld laser rifle at the ready.

"Hey! Grace!" Eric was walking down the driveway nearest her, moving at a fast clip. His voice was low, insistent.

"Eric!" Grace gasped, surprised to see him.

He came close, wrapping his fingers around her arm, drawing her nearer to him.

"There she is!" the officer across the street called to someone. Three more police officers ran out of the house and began running toward Eric and Grace.

Still grasping Grace's arm, Eric took off, propelling her forward.

A stream of electric red crackled past her cheek, scorching a shrub just in front of her. The three G-1 police cut a diagonal path across the street. A blaring truck horn hurt Grace's ears as a large tractor trailer careened onto the road, blocking her view of the approaching police. The truck's brakes screeched as it stopped and the back trailer doors opened.

The young man standing in the tractor trailer looked just like Mfumbe Taylor from the holographic Decode video.

"Go! Go!" Eric urged her to run to the truck. There was no time to think about it — she just had to do it. The young man in the truck reached down to help her up, pulling her in as she jumped up. Eric leaped in beside her.

As they slammed the back doors shut again, another jagged red line buzzed the door handle.

The truck lurched forward, throwing Grace back into its interior. In a moment they were speeding forward. Eric knelt beside her.

"You okay?" he checked.

"I think so. What's happening?" Grace shut her eyes and tried to order the events of the past day and a half as best she could. But they resisted order, or logic. It was a haywire mess, full of jagged holes.

Normal life already seemed like a lifetime ago, like she was now acting out a life that belonged to someone else. At what moment had this new life begun? As the truck raced on, she tried to pinpoint it.

Somehow everything that happened had led to this strange and unlikely moment that she now found herself in — speeding toward somewhere unknown in the back of a tractor trailer.

Wait for my phone call, Dr. Harriman had said. But it was too late for that now. It was too late for her to go home, too late to see if her family had left her any word, any instructions. It was too late to call Emma, too late to do anything without fear of getting someone she loved in trouble.

It was dark in the back of the truck, with scant light trickling in from the outside. She had no sense of where she was anymore, and barely had a sense of who she was with. In the near-dark, she looked at her wrist, tried to make out the details of the Bar Code. But they were as unreadable as anything else about her life. Other people might know the truth of it, but she didn't.

Time passed. She had no sense of how much time. She could have checked her phone, but Eric had taken it from her and immediately dislodged the battery and the info-sim card. He'd thrown the phone forcefully out the back of the truck, then smashed the sim card under his foot, grinding it with the heel of his boot.

"You could have just turned it off," Grace grumbled, upset to see her phone, especially Tilly, so utterly destroyed. For most of her life her Android cell phone had been her link with friends, family, and the world in general. It was on all the time. Grace even slept with it under her pillow. And Tilly, in a crazy way, had become her guide, always tracking her location by satellite so she could direct Grace to the nearest public bathroom, the best restaurant, the closest bank ATM and so much more. Without Tilly's soothing voice, without the phone's comforting connections, Grace felt lost — so lost that her stomach clenched with the stress of it.

"I couldn't just turn it off," Eric said, still standing by the back door of the truck. "It emits a signal even when it's not on. Every part of it does."

The truck swerved just as Eric opened the back door once more and hurled the phone battery out. He grinned, watching it go. "Final level!" he cheered. He turned back to her, still smiling as he latched the door. "Got it right into Hollowbrook Creek. Let them try to find that! As long as that phone is in your possession, off or on, Global-1 can find you."

"Why am I hiding from Global-1 at all?" Grace needed to know. "What's happening?"

"Does it scare you?" Eric asked, ducking the question, in Grace's opinion.

"Yeah, it does," Grace admitted. "Of course I'm scared! I'd be stupid not to be scared."

"Try not to be," Eric advised, "because this is only the start. The wild ride is just beginning."

PART TWO

*Be not afraid of greatness: some are born great,
some achieve greatness, and some have greatness
thrust upon 'em.*

Shakespeare's Twelfth Night, *1602*

SEVEN

When the speeding truck finally stopped, Mfumbe — and she was now certain it was him — opened the door. Eric and Grace jumped down beside him. A woman in her early thirties, dressed in jeans and a T-shirt, descended from the driver's seat and walked toward them.

They were underneath the Los Angeles freeway. The woman introduced herself as Katie and extended her hand to Grace.

Grace shook hands and trained her eyes on the woman's face. "Have we met before?" she asked. The woman looked so familiar and yet she couldn't figure out why.

"You might have seen pictures of me in the papers lately," Katie replied. "They called me Dusa the Drakian Menace in some of the papers, or at least the ones Global-1 owns, which is a lot of them."

"That's it! I saw a story about you on the TV," Grace recalled. About six months earlier, Grace had sat down beside her mother, who was watching the TV report with avid interest. She remembered the reporter explaining that Drakians were an offshoot of Decode, a much more violent group whose illegal tactics violated the law and made its members subject to arrest.

"I know which show you saw," Katie said with a bitter smile that rose up a little higher on the right side of her face than on the left. "It was a batch of lies. We like to mess up Global-1 any chance we get because they keep trying to ruin our lives. But we don't hurt anyone. They didn't even get my name right."

"Your name isn't really Dusa?" Grace asked.

"I called myself Medusa for a while, just to seem scarier to Global-1. It got shortened to Dusa. Then when I thought the bar code tattoo threat was over, I went back to my own name."

Grace clutched the bar code tattoo on her wrist. The lines still tingled and burned slightly. "How is it not over?" she asked. She knew that the events of her own life were somehow tied to this question, even though she couldn't say how.

Eric, Mfumbe, and Katie exchanged anxious glances. "We're not sure, but we think they might be up to something again," Katie answered.

This didn't satisfy Grace at all. But she had more important questions to ask. "What's happened to my family?" Her voice rose with fear. "Why were the police after me?"

"We're not certain of that, either," Katie answered.

"But how did you know to get me?"

"There are people in Global-1 who are sympathetic to our cause," Mfumbe said. "Eric had told us about you, so when your name came up, we knew we had to act decisively."

Every answer was only leading to more questions.

"Who was it?" Grace asked. "On the inside."

Mfumbe shook his head. "We can't tell you. It wouldn't be safe. Not for you. Not for our informants."

As if he could sense her frustration, Eric said gently, "We're still trying to figure most of it out ourselves. The information we got was . . . vague. We need to know your story, too. Why don't you tell us what you know?"

This was a different kind of trust he was asking for now, because it was clear that it would have to be, for the time being, an unequal trust. There were things they couldn't tell her. But at the same time, they needed to know everything.

"Please," Eric said. "We're on your side."

Grace decided to trust him.

"This has to do with it being your birthday," Katie said once Grace had finished her story about Dr. Harriman and about the police coming to her house. When Grace had said Dr. Harriman's name, she had hoped there would be a flash of recognition, a confirmation that he was the one who'd tipped them off. But they hadn't betrayed a thing.

"My birthday?" Grace echoed. "Why should that matter?"

"You'd better come with us," Eric suggested. "There are some people you should meet."

"Eric, I'm really scared. What's this about?" Grace asked.

"There's no reason to be scared," Eric assured her. "For what it's worth, I won't leave your side. Unless, of course, you ask me to."

Katie disappeared into the back of the tractor trailer and came back wheeling a motorcycle with two helmets strapped to it. "I have to get this rig out of here," she explained. "It's not exactly easy to hide this thing. In case I get stopped, I don't want them to find you. Eric, take her to the garage."

"Sure," Eric agreed as Katie and Mfumbe put down the truck's back ramp and wheeled the motorcycle down. "Ever ridden on one of these?" he asked Grace.

She shook her head. She was nervous but excited to try it. With the way her day was going, what harm was a motorcycle ride going to do?

Eric handed her one of the helmets. "Climb on behind me and hang on tight to my waist," he advised.

"See ya back at the ranch," Katie said as she and Mfumbe returned to the truck's cab.

"The ranch?" Grace asked. "For real?"

"She's kidding," Eric explained. "You'll see."

The truck pulled away. Grace and Eric followed and were soon zooming down the roadway. Grace clenched her eyes shut and her arms ached from holding Eric so tightly. Although she'd always wanted to ride a motorcycle, she never thought she'd really get the opportunity. Her parents would never have allowed it. The experience was thrilling and terrifying all at once.

After three blocks, she dared to open her eyes and observe the buildings going by as Eric zipped around corners, eventually turning into an alley between two skyscrapers. At the end of it, a wide garage door stood open. They pulled inside.

Electronic doors closed behind them and the floor they were on began to descend. Grace realized they were inside a large elevator car that was transporting them several levels underground. Finally the car elevator clanked to a jarring stop.

The wall opposite the one they'd entered through opened, revealing an immense underground parking garage. Eric revved the engine and drove slowly into the cavernous space, which was filled with cars, vans, and trucks, including several tractor trailers.

"Where are we?" Grace asked as soon as she and Eric had pulled off their helmets. The elevator left their floor and then returned with Katie and Mfumbe in the truck.

"This is your all-purpose hideout," Eric said with a grin. "Katie calls it the ranch. Decode trackers can't find us under here because we're too deep underground."

"If a meteor were to hit Earth, do you think we would be safe down here?" Grace questioned, looking around at the immense, dank space with its gray walls and exposed pipes. Every so often the news report about the meteor would pop, unbidden and random, into her head. She wasn't really worried about it; she simply couldn't get it completely off her mind.

"What?" Eric asked.

Grace smiled wryly. "Sorry. It's strange, but in the middle of all this craziness, I can't stop thinking about the meteor that's supposed to be heading our way."

"It's supposed to pass us, isn't it?" Eric answered.

"That's what they're saying," Grace agreed.

Eric chuckled with a dark amusement. "I think we have enough other things to worry about right now."

"Absolutely, but are we deep enough underground to be safe?"

"We're deep enough to block a satellite signal. That's all I know," Eric said. "Don't worry about the meteor. It seems like there's one flying by every few years."

A young woman approached them, walking from across the garage. Grace immediately knew who she was — how could she not? It may have been illegal to have the poster of Kayla Reed openly displayed, because President Waters had declared her an enemy of the state. Still, her image was everywhere, and Grace would recognize the eighteen-year-old's lean, high-boned face anywhere.

Kayla and Mfumbe faced each other and held hands, clearly a couple. Kayla lay her forehead on Mfumbe's chest and shut her eyes, as did he. They stood that way for several beats without moving.

"What's that about?" Grace asked Eric.

"They're telepaths," Eric explained. "The early bar code resisters learned to speak with their minds. Many of them still communicate that way."

"Can you do that?" Grace was afraid the answer would be yes.

"No. It takes too much training. I'd rather be climbing."

Grace covered her tattooed wrist with her other hand, suddenly ashamed even though the tattoo was supposed to be safe now. It suddenly felt all wrong to be bar coded here in the presence of these resisters.

Lifting her head, Kayla caught Grace's movement and smiled warmly. "It's all right," she said, brushing back her chin-length light brown hair as she broke away from Mfumbe and approached. "You didn't know, and we didn't get to you in time."

"I didn't know what?" Grace asked.

"You didn't know not to get the tattoo," Kayla replied.

Grace waited for Eric to tell Kayla that he had, in fact, warned her. But he kept quiet, kept this secret for her.

Katie and Mfumbe walked toward them. Glancing at her companions, Grace saw that they all wore bar code tattoos on their wrists. "I don't understand," she said.

"Oh, this?" Kayla took a plastic bottle of clear mineral oil and a cloth from the large satchel she had slung across her chest. She held out her wrist and poured oil from the bottle onto her tattoo, rubbing it with a cloth. Her wrist was instantly smeared black.

"Hey, those things don't grow on trees, you know!" Katie objected.

Kayla spoke as she continued rubbing away her tattoo. "I need a new press-on. This fake is shot," she explained calmly. "There's no more money in the bank account attached to it, and when I tried to use it today, the scanner came up reading DECEASED."

"Are you kidding?" Mfumbe asked. Distressed, he inspected his own tattoo nervously.

"No joke."

"That is seriously banged out," Eric murmured.

This is beyond banged out, Grace thought. Yesterday — this morning — she was working at GlobalHelix headquarters. And now she was in an underground parking garage with the leaders of Decode. Because of years and years of Global-1 messaging, the constant alerts and info blasts the corporation sent to her cell phone, she knew what she was supposed to do: Play along, get information, then turn them in.

Could she do that? Grace felt as though every circuit in her brain was suddenly cross-wired. She liked these people. They spoke to her as though she were one of them. And Eric was one of them, after all. She'd admired him for so long. He was a hero in her school — not to mention this attraction that was between them lately. How could she turn him in?

The answer was that she couldn't.

Maybe she should just try to get away and not mention them. She could say she was blindfolded or knocked out. But first she had to find out what was going on.

Katie had crossed the wide aisle and climbed into the cab of a tractor trailer. Sitting in the driver's seat with the door open, she took a metal box from the passenger side and opened it. "This one should be good for a while," she said, handing Kayla a delicate piece of plastic, resembling cellophane tape, with a bar code imprinted on it.

Kayla took a facecloth from her pack and wet it at a nearby water fountain. Pressing the flexible plastic to her inner wrist, she put the damp cloth over it. When she lifted the cloth, a new bar code tattoo was there on her wrist.

Grace looked to Eric with a questioning expression. "Is your bar code tattoo a fake also?" she asked.

Eric nodded. "We all have fakes."

"Why didn't you tell me this the other night when we were talking about it?" She remembered how tentative he'd seemed, as though he wanted to reveal something but had decided against it.

"Grace, I didn't know what to do. I wasn't sure I wanted to involve you in all this."

"Well, I'm involved now," Grace said.

"I know. I'm sorry." Eric's apology was so sincere it seemed to hurt him. "There are a lot of things I didn't realize then that I know now."

"Like what?" Grace demanded.

"We'll tell you everything we know in a minute," Katie cut in. Then she turned to Kayla and said, "We'd better tell Jack about your bum fake. That shouldn't have happened."

"Is he here?" Kayla asked.

"He's in the back with Allyson," Mfumbe said. "They've been here all day making changes on the swing-lo."

"Let's go talk to him about this," Katie suggested. "We'll be right back," she added, turning to Eric and Grace.

"The swing-lo?" Grace asked Eric as the others walked toward the far end of the garage.

"This garage is where they build them," he answered.

"But what is it?"

"It's this cool flying saucer that this guy from Ireland, Jack Kelly, invented. Some mysterious billionaire is funding the thing, so Jack and his business partner, Allyson Minor, are working to get them into production."

"Why do the others have to talk to them about the fake tattoos?"

"Jack is a genius computer hacker and he works with Decode," Eric explained. "I heard he's been writing advanced computer code from the time he was eleven — and he never even went to college. He's the one who hacks into bank and government files and gets out the information on people who have passed away. A lot of times the dead people have left bank accounts with unclaimed funds in them. Jack is able to convert this info into bar code form and doctor it so the birth dates seem current."

"So your bar code tattoo has the name of a dead person in it?" Grace asked.

"Yeah," Eric replied. "It's not foolproof, but as long as nobody is paying close attention, it enables us to buy stuff and not get arrested for walking around without a bar code."

Eric took Grace's hand. All at once, she felt electrified by his touch and soothed by the strength and firmness of his grip. "Come on," he said gently. "I'll show you the swing-lo. It's final level. You'll like it."

He led her in the direction that the others had gone. Clusters of people were gathered in different sections of the garage. They spoke in low tones and their discussions appeared serious. Some individuals slept in sleeping bags inside the parked cars, others curled up on the hoods. They looked up sleepily as Eric and Grace passed. A few nodded to Eric, acknowledging that they'd seen him before.

"Who are these people?" Grace asked quietly.

"Some Decode, mostly Drakians."

"Why do they call themselves Drakians?" Grace asked.

"They admire Gene Drake, the tattooer who got shot for refusing to do more tattoos. The Global-1 cops claimed he was threatening people lined up for the tattoo, but he wasn't. He and a friend had hacked their way into the Global-1 database and knew that the company was encoding genetics and injecting nanobots. They killed him so he could never tell. They claimed his friend killed himself, but I doubt it. They murdered him."

Again, Grace felt torn between what she was being told now and what she'd been told for the rest of her life. In the Global-1 version of events, the Drakians were the murderers, stopping at nothing to overthrow order. And looking around, there was something a little disconcerting about their presence — these were not people with jobs, not people with families who lived in houses and paid mortgages. They were so outside the margins, she wondered how they could judge what was in the margins. Especially if they backed their judgment with violence.

But she couldn't say any of this to Eric, could she? Not here. She knew she was supposed to feel safe, but she didn't. She couldn't. It was all too new.

It was unnerving to think that these people knew about her. Kayla had said Grace's name had come up. Why? How? There was so much more she needed to find out. The most important question, of course, was her family's whereabouts. They'd left so fast that they couldn't even wait for her! Did they think she'd be better off on her own? Grace knew her parents would never simply take off without serious thought to her welfare. They just weren't like that.

"Hey, Eric, is that her?" asked a guy who had been reading a newspaper, sprawled across the hood of his car.

Eric gave the guy a quick wave. "Mission accomplished," he replied.

"Final level!" the guy cheered. Others looked up and there was a wave of applause and cheering.

"Welcome to our home sweet home, Grace!" a young woman called.

Grace nodded and smiled uncomfortably. "Do they all know my name?" Grace whispered to Eric.

"Pretty much," Eric confirmed. "Drakians pride themselves on constantly knowing things. They have a really great underground spy network. Some of them may look like bums, but a lot of them come from wealthy families, and their parents are super connected. They get top level information just by being around their homes once in a while."

"And what about the others?" Grace asked.

Eric smiled, as though her question amused him. "They're bums."

"No. Really?"

"Yeah, really. But street people hear things, too, important things."

"And nobody minds that they're here?" was the most Grace could think to ask. "Do they live here?"

"Hard to say. They come and they go. No one questions it. The same guy who funds the swing-lo owns this garage. He's completely mysterious. The guys Jack and Allyson speak to are just agents for the guy with the money. He thinks Jack and Allyson are just using the space for their swing-lo business, but since they're also Decode operatives, Jack and Allyson let us operate out of here."

They came to a spot where Katie, Kayla, and Mfumbe stood talking to a young man and woman — Grace assumed they were Jack and Allyson. Behind them sat something large and mechanical covered with a bright blue tarp. Grace guessed it must be the swing-lo, though what a swing-lo was, she still had no real idea.

Jack appeared to be in his early twenties, of medium height, with deep blue eyes. Grace couldn't help but be struck by his movie-star good looks.

Allyson's most striking feature was her halo of shoulder-length blond curls. Although she was heavier than was fashionable, she had an appealing, open face.

"Someone has out-hacked us," Jack said raking his hand through his shaggy-cut blond hair. "That's got to be the only answer."

"Why *my* fake and no one else's?" Kayla questioned.

"Because you're the most well-known bar code resister. Your story has been all over the papers. Naturally they would look for your fake first," Jack deduced. "It's got to be Global-1 that's doing this."

"They probably haven't gotten access to every fake," Allyson suggested hopefully. She turned to Kayla. "Have the K clones complained of bad fakes?"

"I haven't heard from them lately," Kayla replied.

Once again, Grace could hardly believe this was happening. It amazed her that she should find herself among these people she had read about.

Six months earlier Grace had perused a magazine article on Kayla and her five clones, who were like twins, but not exactly, because each of them was increasingly transgenic. Their genes had been spliced with those of sparrows. Kayla was called K-1, with the least amount of bird gene. The one they called Karen was K-6. Heavily autistic and disheveled looking, she had never left the GlobalHelix complex until Kayla and the others liberated her; Karen was the one who had memorized the algorithms that shut down the nanobots controlled by the bar code tattoo.

Jack noticed Grace and Eric for the first time and smiled. "Hey, Eric, who's your friend?"

"It's her, Jack," Katie said before Eric could introduce Grace. "She's the one we've been telling you about, the one our informant told us to pick up. She's in big trouble."

Big trouble? Grace wished someone would give her an answer to what was happening.

Kayla nodded, turning toward Grace. "It sounds like they're onto you, Grace."

What were they talking about? "Me? Who's onto me?"

"Global-1, of course," Mfumbe told her. "They've been waiting for you to turn seventeen for a long time. Something big is going to go down now."

"Why?" Grace said.

But it was as if she hadn't said anything.

"Do you really think this is it?" Kayla asked him.

Mfumbe nodded his head emphatically and spread his arms wide in a gesture that said it should be obvious. "It's all in the prophecy."

Katie shot Mfumbe a hard look of disapproval. Grace realized he had said something in front of her that Katie hadn't wanted revealed.

Prophecy?

"Why can't she know?" Mfumbe challenged Katie. "She's as deeply involved in this as any of us."

"Not the prophecy. Not yet," Katie spoke in a low tense tone that was almost a growl.

Mfumbe turned his back to her and began walking away. "We're never going to see eye to eye on this, Katie. It's just that simple."

Grace longed to ask what this was about, but the atmosphere was so tense she couldn't find the nerve. Not anymore.

True to his word, Eric was still at her side. She didn't know how to interpret his silence. Did he know what they were talking about? If so, was he going to tell her later?

"Mfumbe has a good point," Kayla said to Katie.

"Don't defend him just because the two of you are together," Katie snapped.

Kayla drew back, offended by the comment. "That's not true and you know it! How can she help us with The Bar Code Prophecy if we don't tell her about it?

"Not yet!" Katie insisted. "*Not yet.*"

"All right." Kayla turned to Grace. "We're going to tell you about the prophecy. I promise. But there are equally important things you need to know first."

"Like what?" Grace asked. At this point she felt so far over her head that more complex questions seemed beside the point.

"Global-1 has found out you're adopted. They're after your biological father and that's why they're looking for you."

EIGHT

Grace felt as though she were in a dream as she listened to Kayla speak. A bad dream. "Adopted? What are you talking about?"

"You didn't know?" Kayla asked.

"I don't believe you," Grace murmured. She could feel Eric getting closer behind her, backing her with his presence, the rope now invisible between them. He put his hand gently but firmly on her arm, and she was grateful for the support. She hadn't seen this coming and she felt almost faint from the impact.

"I know this is messing with your head," Kayla said to Grace. "You must be feeling the way I did when I discovered I was one of six clones and that I share genes with an actual bird."

Grace acknowledged the comparison with a nod, but she didn't really feel this was the same. And just because Kayla had been through something similar didn't mean this wasn't weird. No, not weird. Earth-shattering.

"So you're saying that my family isn't my family?" Grace asked in an unsteady voice.

"Of course they're your family," Allyson spoke kindly. "But you don't share their genetics. That's all."

"Lots of people are adopted," Eric added softly.

"Yes, but they grow up knowing it. They don't learn it abruptly from strangers at seventeen," Grace objected, fighting the tears that were welling up. And then a sudden memory hit her, changing everything. "Wait a minute! Why are you lying to me?"

"We're not," Kayla insisted. "You were adopted by your parents at birth."

"My parents have a DVD of my birth. I've *seen* it!"

"I can't explain that, Grace," Kayla admitted.

"All we know is what Decode headquarters has told us," Mfumbe added.

"I'm sorry to have dumped that on you so clumsily," Kayla apologized. Mfumbe returned to the group and stood beside Kayla, resting his hand on her shoulder. "It didn't occur to me that you might not know about your adoption," she added. "I'm sorry."

Grace didn't believe it. They had to be mistaken. "So, basically, you want me to take it *on faith* that I'm adopted, just because Decode headquarters — wherever and whoever that is — tells you so? Can you understand that I might need a little more proof than that?"

"We have our sources and spies and computer hackers just like Global-1 does. We have to, in order to fight them," Jack said. "The moment you got the bar code tattoo, your DNA flooded into the Global-1 data banks. Apparently they were just waiting for it. You're the child of someone very important to them. They've been watching you and so have we, because we're hacked into their newsfeed and we can follow whatever they're following."

"I get it. Global-1 is evil because of all their surveillance. And then, wait, you go and do the same exact thing?" Grace was angry now, and it felt liberating. "So you sent someone to stalk me. Great. Whoever it was did a great job. I had no idea."

"It was me, Grace," Eric said.

His words hit her, battered her. For a moment, she didn't have enough air in her lungs to speak.

"You?" she stammered dryly when her voice returned. She'd never felt so *foolish*. "Wow," she said with a note of sarcasm. "And all this time I thought we were friends." And had hoped they were *more* than friends.

"We *are* friends," Eric insisted, but Grace felt too betrayed to believe him.

"Whatever you say," Grace muttered dismissively, turning her back on him. "Does anyone know who my biological parents are? Just out of curiosity."

"The file says you were born at GlobalHelix," Katie revealed.

Grace's eyes darted to Kayla. "Am I a clone, too?"

"Probably not," Kayla replied. "My file revealed my clone status."

"There was no information like that in your file," Mfumbe said.

"Then why do they *have* a file on me?" Grace needed to know.

"There's a file on everybody," Jack said. "The thing that made your file important was that it was deeply encrypted. Only the most top secret of all the Global-1 files get that."

"So you have no idea why?" Grace pressed.

What else are you not telling me?

"But we do know that someone has abducted your family — and on the same day you got the bar code tattoo," Katie said with level calm.

Grace realized that the news of being adopted had almost no impact on her, compared to this. Her family was the *only* family she'd ever known. It wasn't a perfect family. But who had that? No one *she* knew.

Why wouldn't they have told her she was adopted? It was puzzling. But if that was a question, there were other things that weren't at all questionable. Her family loved her — even pesky Kim and James — she was certain of that much. And at the moment it was what mattered. She loved her family, they loved her — and something had happened to them.

But the cars. The cars were gone. If they'd been abducted, then why were the cars gone?

"Do you know who's responsible for whatever's happened to them?" Grace asked.

"It's probably Global-1," Mfumbe said. "Either they've abducted them or you're family is on the run from them."

So it was still a possibility that they were on the run.

Ultimately, it seemed that Grace's instincts were as informed as Decode's operation.

"I should go back and tell the police all this," Grace suggested, more to gauge their reaction than anything else.

"Global-1 *owns* the police," Kayla reminded her. "If Global-1 is behind this, the police will never solve your case. And I wouldn't go into any foster home they assign for you, either."

A threat. It was almost too easy — everything that they said Global-1 would do became something that would happen to her if she didn't cooperate with Decode.

As if he realized this, Eric cautioned, "Kayla. We're not going to let that happen to Grace."

Grace couldn't stop herself. "As far as I'm concerned," she told Eric, "you have nothing at all to do with what happens to me. Get it?" Before he could answer, she turned back to Kayla and asked, "Why, what would they do to me?" She figured she might as well have as full a picture as possible.

"You might be the only one of your family they didn't get," Katie reminded her. "At any rate, they know you're not with the rest of your family. They are probably looking for you, too."

"Ironic, isn't it, that you were right there in the GlobalHelix building and they didn't find you?" Jack commented.

"I went home early. The only one I told was Terri, my replacement," Grace recalled.

"Did anyone else see you there?" Katie asked.

"Lots of people work there," Grace replied.

"Who did you talk to?" Kayla asked.

"The tattoo nurse, and Terri," Grace recalled.

"And Dr. Harriman," Mfumbe said.

"Yes — I already told you about him." Grace turned to Kayla, who hadn't been there for her first debriefing. "He's a very strange man. For some reason he was upset that I'd gotten the bar code tattoo."

Grace could tell from the stunned expressions of everyone

around her that she'd said something significant. But what was it?

"You spoke to Jonathan Harriman, the inventor of the bar code tattoo?" Allyson reiterated. "Actually spoke to him? Does he know you?"

"He always remembers my name," Grace said. "But it's not like we've ever had a real conversation. Not until today."

"Can you get in to talk to him tonight?" Kayla asked.

"I have clearance," Grace confirmed, unsure of where this was going. "Although they might have cancelled it."

"I wonder if he's still there," Allyson said. "It's already six."

"I could call Terri," Grace suggested. "The front desk is manned until eight and then it goes to voice mail. I trust her to tell me what's going on."

"Here," Jack said, pulling a phone out of his pocket. "This one's secure."

She punched in the number for the GlobalHelix front desk and waited as the phone rang one, two, three, four, five times. "That's odd," Grace told the others. "We never let the phone ring more than three times."

Grace tried the call again, and this time let it sound seven times, still with no success. "Strange," she remarked, giving up.

"Someone should get out there and see what's going on," Katie suggested.

But Grace wasn't through. There were still things she wanted to know.

"What about the prophecy?" Grace asked. "Can you tell me about that now?"

"After we talk to Jonathan Harriman," Katie replied. "He might have information for us about the prophecy, information about your family. If anyone knows, it's him."

"Hey, Eric," Jack said, turning toward the covered vehicle behind him and gripping the edge of the tarp covering it. "This might be a great chance to take the new swing-lo for a test run."

NINE

"This is it . . . my baby . . . the swing-lo," Jack said as Eric and Grace climbed into the craft. "Of course, Allyson has made a lot of improvements since I showed her the first prototype a while ago. What a piece of junk that was, compared to this one."

"And this one is still not the end product, we hope," Allyson added, joining them. "All these dials and switches have to go. I mean, it's so old-fashioned."

"Hey, I was working with scrap metal out in the desert," Jack defended his design. "I was using car parts. Give me a break."

Allyson smiled and pushed him playfully. "Just saying, we can get something a little slicker going here."

"We're going to have to hit our mysterious business backer for more money before that can happen," Jack replied.

Grace kept her gaze on them and wouldn't look at Eric, who sat beside her in the swing-lo's driver's seat. Her emotions about him were wavering between disappointment, anger, and feelings of betrayal; she'd been so sure he was paying attention to her solely because he returned her feelings. The idea that she was only his *assignment* — that otherwise he wouldn't even have noticed her — was humiliating.

When she looked at him, she felt embarrassed and furious. She couldn't bear to meet his eyes. But she'd been told to ride in the swing-lo with him and meet the others at GlobalHelix. She didn't feel she was in a position to say no. If this is what it would take to get her family and her life back, she couldn't say no.

Grace also held mixed emotions about traveling in the shiny metallic disc in front of her. It had no more than a twelve-foot diameter. At its center was a seat well where two people could sit side by side. In front was a very high-tech computer control panel.

"It works on magnetic repulsion, and it's going to be the next big thing," Jack told Grace. "Eric here is my test pilot."

Jack gave her a quick history of the swing-lo. Although magnetic repulsion had been around for a while — high speed trains in Japan ran on it, as did the Bullit-Buses and Bullit-Trains in America and Europe — he had done something no one else had yet managed to do. He had amplified the force so that his swing-lo could actually fly.

"This idea of personal flying vehicles isn't new," Allyson added. "Guys like the physicist Nikola Tesla were working on it back in the early nineteen hundreds. He even had funding from John Jacob Astor and everything. They predicted it was how people would commute, but they never made it work. Now, over a hundred years later, we think we've got it."

"It's just a tiny bit unreliable," Jack admitted with a quick grimace. "But we're almost there."

"In what way unreliable?" Grace asked nervously.

"You'll be safe," Allyson assured her. "We're just playing around with the altitude."

"Put this on and make sure you're belted in," Eric said when they sat side by side in the vehicle. He handed her the same helmet she'd worn on the motorcycle.

Kayla, Mfumbe, and Katie headed back to their own motorcycles, but Allyson and Jack remained, watching as Eric switched on a series of buttons and toggles. "This is prototype five," Eric told Grace, speaking in a friendly tone, as though nothing was strained between them. "You should have seen the first one; it looked like a hunk of junk because Jack had only scrap metal to work with. Now with the funding, he can buy some decent lightweight materials."

"I should be out looking for my family, not fooling around with some spaceship," Grace fretted. She knew there was supposed to be an element of fun in all this. But what right did she have to be on an adventure like this when they were missing?

"We *are* searching for them," Eric said. "We're going to see what Jonathan Harriman can tell us. He said he would contact you, right? Well, there's no way for him to do that now. So we have to do it for him. You'll get around a lot faster with us than on your own. And if you relied on the Global-1 cops . . . believe me, you'd get nowhere."

Eric pushed another button and the swing-lo elevated abruptly to about five feet off the ground. Jack and Allyson came alongside. "We've made some big innovations, Eric. You can put the roof bubble up now and she goes a lot higher. There's a gauge to the right that will tell your elevation above sea level. If you get the chance, see how high she'll go."

"How high is too high?" Eric asked as he strapped on his helmet.

"We don't know," Allyson admitted. "But the craft will start to shake when you're too high."

"Oh, swell," Eric quipped sarcastically.

"Just bring it back down and the shimmying will stop," Jack assured him. "But don't keep it shaking too long."

"Why? What will happen?" Eric asked.

"Just don't do it and everything will be fine," Jack insisted.

With a nod to Jack and Allyson, Eric pushed the throttle forward and the swing-lo whirred forward, traveling toward the wide garage door from which they had entered. Grace gripped her seat anxiously. She found it strange to be traveling so close to the ground, and yet not be touching the earth.

The garage door had been opened, and now the craft entered. Immediately the doors shut and the elevator car began traveling upward. When it bumped to a stop, the door on the opposite side opened. Eric turned on headlights that illuminated the area around them. Instead of using the narrow alley the motorcycle had come down on the trip in, Eric steered to the left and came out into a gated children's playground.

"Going up," Eric warned as the swing-lo lifted above the fence and sailed over it. "Jack's big invention is a mechanism that amplifies the magnetic repulsion coming from the earth many times over," he explained. "It's a totally clean fuel, and the thing can really fly."

Grace nodded as she peered over the side. As long as they were talking about the machine, she could bear the sound of his voice. But that was about it. They were flying at about ten feet in the air, still needing to stay to the roadways rather than flying above buildings. "We're heading down again," Eric reported. "If I stay close to the road, people just think this a funky new car, some kind of experimental hybrid. They don't even notice that the thing isn't actually on the ground, especially now that it's dark."

They traveled toward GlobalHelix without talking any further. At one point Grace spied Mfumbe, Kayla, and Katie riding ahead of them. Eric flew up and buzzed them from above before speeding past.

After twenty minutes, they turned the corner toward GlobalHelix. Grace looked at Eric directly for the first time since learning the truth about their relationship.

"What?" he asked.

"I didn't say anything," she pointed out.

"That scowl on your face did, though," Eric countered. "What's wrong? Is my driving making you sick?"

"No," Grace replied. "You lied to me. Why didn't you tell me what was going on?"

"I wanted to, Grace, but I couldn't. I wouldn't have been doing my job if I had. You can understand that, can't you?"

"Yes. You were just *doing your job*. How could I not understand that?" Grace replied. "Still . . . I thought we were friends."

"We *are* friends," Eric insisted as he slowed the swing-lo in front of the Global-1 headquarters. "I'm going over this gate so I can park the swing-lo inside, then your code will get us in the front door."

"If it works," Grace said.

"Yeah. If it works."

Once more the swing-lo rose and easily sailed over the wall before descending on the lawn outside the headquarters. Low amber lights glowed from the lobby. There was no sign of activity inside. They left the craft stashed behind some forsythia bushes and headed for the front entrance.

Grace ran her new bar code tattoo across the front door scanner.

ACCESS DENIED.

"Maybe it's too soon. I'll try the eye scan."

ACCESS DENIED.

"You've been wiped clean. They're not admitting you anymore. Can you think of another way in?"

"There's a door on the roof that isn't scanner protected, but it's usually locked."

Eric's eyes darted to the swing-lo and back to Grace. "Want to try it?"

"Can it go that high?"

"We'll find out."

Grace gazed up at the huge spiral sculpture on the roof. Looking up was vastly preferable to looking down. She had never been frightened of heights, but as the aircraft rose, it began to shimmy, first just slightly. But the higher they went, the more violent the shaking became.

"Don't worry, Jack has landed on this roof before," Eric said, though his expression was not confident. "And that was with the first swing-lo."

Grace kept her eyes fixed on the twisting sculpture and remembered what she'd learned in biology: the double helix represented a spiral polymer of nucleic acids held together by nucleotides that base-paired together. It was how genetic information was stored and copied. Genetics was what Global-1 was all about. It had started as a company that made hybrid food and grew to one that made animal clones for meat production. Now it was trying to make hybrid people. And it was doing everything in its power to control the population, just as they had cornered the market on the world's food supply. *We're just a product to them, like cattle,* Grace had seen Ambrose Young quoted as saying in a recent article — the image had stuck with her, even though she'd thought at the time it was overblown. Now she considered it in a different light as the swing-lo rose ever higher.

What's Genetics Got to Do with It?

Article by Allyson Minor
Reporting from the California Institute of Technology

GMO: genetically modified organism. All your fruits and vegetables are genetically modified. As far back as the early 2000s Global-1, acting under the company names of its subsidiaries, was granted patents on its hybridized foods. In the 2010s, it filed for and received patents for its cloned sheep, cattle, and pigs. These were then used not only as meat for consumption but also as living tissue for its organ cloning programs. Maybe you've seen the famous photo of the rat with a human ear growing from its spine. And then Global-1 turned its attention to you.

That's right: you. And all your human friends and family. How would it be if you could fly? Or see in the dark? It might be cool. It might save lives.

The problem is that Global-1 thinks that since it is going to such huge expense to develop these technologies that could improve you — just as they believe they've improved the tomato and the pig — they should also have a patent on you.

Put simply, Global-1 wants to own you.

And it practically does.

It has already branded almost all of us who are seventeen and over with its bar code tattoo. I resisted for a while but gave in so I could enter college. I was suspicious but even I didn't know that my genetic information was being studied and stored within the lines of the Bar Code or that nanobots introduced into my bloodstream during the tattooing process were adding a machine component that could be manipulated by Global-1 at will.

The brave individuals who have been able to resist the bar code tattoo and who have exposed these outrages to the public are not convinced that the danger has been resolved. Despite calls for his resignation, Loudon Waters, the Global-1 pawn, is still our president. The bar code tattoo continues to be the law of the land.

"We're just a product to them, like cattle," Ambrose Young has told the Senate.

But why would the government listen to resistors? If we are cattle to Global-1, then the government is a herd of sheep.

Decode remains committed to guarding your freedom. Support them in any way you can. When you meet a Postman — the Decode organization that works to keep you communicating off the grid — ask how you can help.

TEN

Eric and Grace sped lightly down the dimly lit top floor of the GlobalHelix offices. The roof door had been locked, but luckily it was an old-fashioned lock, and among the few items Eric carried in a backpack was a lock-picking kit.

Once they were inside, they headed down a flight of stairs to an executive suite of offices. It was strange for Grace to think that just this morning, she worked here. She pointed at the line of light emanating from under the door of Dr. Harriman's office. She'd never been inside it, but she knew where it was.

"He's still here," she whispered to Eric.

Or at least she hoped so. It could also be a trap.

There was only one way to find out.

"Dr. Harriman?" Grace inquired as she opened the door.

Dr. Harriman looked up sharply from the laptop on his desk. He did not look happy to see her.

"Grace! What are you doing here?"

"I need to talk to you. You're the inventor of the bar code tattoo. Do you know why there is a priority file on me?"

"Well, you're certainly a direct young woman."

"I have to be. My family is missing. I'm trying to find them and I can't afford to wait."

It was as if Grace could see his scientific mind weighing the options. "Maybe I do know something about it," he hedged. "Who is your friend?"

Eric stepped forward. "My name is Eric Chaca."

"You're Native American?" Dr. Harriman inquired.

Grace thought this was a strange thing to say, but Eric seemed to know why Dr. Harriman was asking. "My father is half Hopi, half Irish," he answered. "My mother is full Cherokee."

"Have you come to talk to me about The Bar Code Prophecy?"

Grace turned toward Eric — *the prophecy, again* — but Eric wasn't paying any attention to her. Instead he and Dr. Harriman were locked in a meaningful stare.

"I didn't come for that," Eric said. "I had no idea you knew anything about it."

"But *you* know about it, don't you?" Dr. Harriman said.

Nodding slowly, Eric approached Dr. Harriman. "First things first," he told the older man. "Why is there a top priority file on Grace?"

Dr. Harriman's ice blue eyes darted thoughtfully between Grace and Eric. Grace's heartbeat quickened with anticipation.

"There is a special top priority file on Grace Morrow because she is the daughter of the inventor of the bar code tattoo."

"Your daughter?" Grace spoke softly as the impact of his words struck her.

"My daughter," Dr. Harriman confirmed.

Now it was she and Dr. Harriman who studied each other with keen eyes, each searching for physical features that might connect them. There was nothing Grace could see. Where his eyes were bright blue, hers were a deep brown, like her hair. But slowly she realized that the shape of her eyes and line of her eyebrows were the same. She owed the ridge of her cheekbone to him, too.

"The darker gene often dominates," Dr. Harriman remarked, as if reading her thoughts. "But I see much of myself in you."

"Why didn't you want her to get the bar code tattoo?" Eric asked while Grace stayed almost frozen, finding it hard to absorb this shocking new piece of information.

"I'd like to explain all this to you someday, but there's something you should look at right away." Dr. Harriman beckoned for them to come around his desk and look at his monitor screen.

Global-1 police swarmed the bottom floor lobby.

"What's going on?" Eric asked, alarmed.

"They arrived just minutes ago. They want me but I'm sure they'd be delighted to take you two, as well," Dr. Harriman explained calmly. "So far I've locked off the executive elevators and the emergency stairways, but I'm sure they'll figure some way up eventually." He looked at them sharply as a new idea occurred to him. "By the way, how did you two manage it?"

The deafening flap of helicopter blades suddenly roared around them. It sounded like more than one. "Drone helicopters," Dr. Harriman observed. "I once wanted to be a helicopter pilot. Now the profession doesn't even exist. It's all drones."

"Why do they want you?" Grace asked. "You work for Global-1. Aren't you on their side?"

"It seems I've turned renegade on them," Dr. Harriman explained. "No longer cooperative."

The chopper blades were growing louder.

"We should go," Eric said.

"How are you proposing we leave?" Dr. Harriman asked.

"We're in a flying craft that takes only two," Eric said. "I'm afraid we have to leave without you."

"I saw a photo of it online," Dr. Harriman said. "I read that it was used when this building was attacked just six months ago. Can't I squeeze in?"

"Come on, let's go, Grace," Eric urged, taking her hand and pulling her along. "Sorry, Dr. Harriman, there's only room for two."

But you should take him, Grace thought. After all, Harriman was the prize. He was the one Decode would want. Grace was nobody.

Still, Eric had made his choice. And he wasn't going back.

Together they ran back to the roof door. The moment they pulled it open, gale force winds assaulted them, stirred up by the two drone helicopters over their heads.

Staggering under the wind of the whirring blades, they ran under the blinding lights from above, crouching toward the swing-lo. A line of red appeared inches from Grace's feet and she followed its line to its source — the helicopter nearest them. "Laser stun!" Eric shouted over the thunderous roar.

At the swing-lo, they dove inside. Eric activated the engine but didn't turn on the lights. Immediately the craft began to rise. It was four feet in the air when a man's hand grabbed the side. Dr. Harriman was trying to climb in.

Acting on an impulse not to leave him stranded, Grace seized Dr. Harriman's arm and began to pull. Another line of red pinged off the side of the swing-lo, raising sparks.

"He's too heavy for us to carry!" Eric shouted.

"We can't leave him out here like this!" Grace countered, gripping Dr. Harriman. It took all her strength to pull him in, his legs still dangling over the edge.

The swing-lo weaved wildly. Grace clutched the scientist, terrified that he might fall.

Red laser lines crossed the dark night.

Eric regained control of the craft and flew horizontally to the right, staying below the helicopters. There was a moment's respite in the laser attacks, and it seemed they had outrun the helicopters or at least eluded them in the dark.

Grace craned her neck around Dr. Harriman. Although she could not see the copters' lights, Grace could still hear them. They sounded close.

Suddenly they rose on either side of the swing-lo, their lights nearly blinding. Eric pulled back on the throttle and the craft rose abruptly above the helicopters. The red lasers sparked on the sides. Pulling the throttle to the right, Eric sent the craft speeding horizontally, creating a distance between it and the copters. "We're going dark," Eric announced as he shut the swing-lo's lights and flew out of the beams coming from the helicopters.

The shaking that Grace had noticed earlier was now very strong. Eric drove the craft toward the tops of some trees. Their speed increased tremendously and Grace looked to Eric for an explanation. "I'm riding an air current," he explained. "It's pushing us along like a wave."

The swing-lo was suddenly flung upward with amazing force. "We just collided with one of the helicopters!" Eric explained. "I think they're cloaked."

"Do you mean invisible?" Grace asked.

Eric nodded. "Stealth technology."

"They are cloaked," Dr. Harriman confirmed. "I developed the technology for Global-1 myself."

"Hang on!" Eric told them. "I want to go higher into this fog to get away from them." When they had climbed steeply, the craft hung in the air a moment and then began to shake violently,

"What's happening?" Dr. Harriman demanded.

"We're too high!" Eric announced pointing to the gauge, which read *1000 feet*. He reached under his seat and pulled out a nylon bag the size of a backpack. "There's one under your seat, Grace," he said. "Give it to the doc. You and I will share."

Rummaging under her feet, Grace withdrew a nylon bag identical to the one Eric held. "What is it?"

The sounds of cracking metal made them all turn toward the jagged tear at the side of the swing-lo.

"Parachutes," Eric replied, pulling open his sack.

"But it's pitch black out there!" Dr. Harriman cried.

"Just put it on, Doc," Eric insisted.

The swing-lo rattled even more violently. "Put this on, Grace," Eric said, handing Grace a harness. "You're going to clip on to me."

"Listen, Doc, we're low to do a sky dive," Eric instructed as he and Grace got into their halters. "Pull the rip cord right away, as soon as you jump." He showed Dr. Harriman where to pull.

"Grace, as we exit, tuck your chin and try to arch your back," Eric explained, speaking with rapid urgency. "Don't be scared. You'll be clipped to me."

Eric attached Grace to his harness just as, with a horrific sound of tearing metal, the swing-lo ripped apart, its pieces disappearing into the night.

Suddenly there was nothing beneath Grace's feet. She wanted to scream but the tremendous force of the wind blowing into her face snatched away her breath. They were falling through the night sky.

Grace was too amazed to be terrified.

How was this happening to her? She was high up in the black night, free-falling rapidly through the sky.

Then all, at once, with a tremendous whoosh, the chute opened over her head and she was floating, drifting toward the earth below.

ELEVEN

Grace opened her eyes and, in the first soft light of morning, saw Eric asleep a few feet away, his nylon backpack at his side. She sat up quickly, alarmed and confused about how she'd gotten into this field of dense tall reeds. And what was she sitting on?

The nylon parachute beneath them snapped memory back to her: The wild feeling of falling through the night sky; her immense relief when the parachute opened; the hard rolling landing, tangled in the lines and nylon of the chute. Finally they had staggered into this field of high stalks and grasses and collapsed in this small clearing, grateful to be alive.

Her last memory was of watching the lights of the two cloaked drone helicopters fly off, having abandoned their pursuit.

Assuming, no doubt, they had died in the crash.

Standing, Grace searched for Dr. Harriman but didn't see him — though in this high grass he might be asleep just yards away. Opening her mouth, she was about to call to him, but decided that she didn't want to wake Eric. Not yet, anyway.

Grace needed time alone to think about everything that had happened in the last twenty-four hours.

There was so much to absorb, to try to make sense of.

She was adopted. That was okay. Her family was still her

family, the only family she'd ever known. But it might explain some of the differences she'd always been so aware of — why she was the only one who was good at math, including her parents; why she was the only one of them who was athletic and had no fear of heights; and probably why she alone was slim while the others tended to be shorter and rounder.

All at once Grace knew who she looked like: Dr. Harriman. But with brown eyes. So who was this brown-eyed birth mother of hers?

Grace remembered Kayla's story of being part of an experiment. Mfumbe had said there was nothing like that in her file . . . but still, it seemed possible. She would insist that Dr. Harriman tell her everything. He owed her that now. She had saved him from the Global-1 cops.

Turning her gaze to Eric, she felt less angry at him, not as betrayed. It was just that she had liked him so much and had loved thinking he returned the attraction. She could deal with this new relationship though. He was a good guy and she was glad he was around. She felt safer with him. She would never be able to trust him completely — but maybe she could trust him enough. He hadn't left her stranded at GlobalHelix when he should have taken Dr. Harriman instead of taking her. That said something about his feelings for her, at least.

"Grace?" Eric rubbed his eyes as he sat up. "Are you okay?"

"No broken bones," she reported.

"Boy, you have a lot of guts," Eric praised her.

It brought a smile to her lips. "Thanks."

"Are you all right? I have some first aid stuff in my pack if you need it."

Grace was aware of her stinging arm that had become scraped when she landed, but the pain wasn't too bad. "I'll be all right. How are you?"

"Still in one piece," he reported. "You've had some day, huh? How's your head?"

"Spinning," Grace admitted.

"No kidding," he sympathized. Eric stood and checked the area. "No sign of Harriman. I hope he made it down okay."

It hadn't occurred to Grace that Dr. Harriman might not have survived the jump. "We should look for him," she said urgently. "He might be hurt."

"You stay here and call out to him. If we get separated in this tall grass, we might never find each other again."

"We can find each other; we have our phones," Grace said out of habit. She could always find her friends in crowds when they each had their phones — which was always. Ever since she could strap her bendable phone around her wrist, Grace even slept with it.

Grace checked her wrist, and the image of Eric tossing it, in pieces, out the back of the speeding truck came back to her.

Eric raised his eyebrows, shrugged, and grinned at her reaction.

As the realization of her phoneless state returned to her, Grace frowned deeply. It was disconcerting not to have her phone and she felt terribly vulnerable without it. She had never before worried about being lost. With Tilly always crooning directions in her ear and friends only a finger glide away, she was never lost. It was as if she'd suddenly gone back in time to some long-ago past when people lived without being able to always contact each other.

"You'd be in a Global-1 police station right now if you had your phone," Eric reminded her.

Grace wondered if that would have been so bad, but Eric and the others seemed convinced that it would be. So did Dr. Harriman.

Eric pulled his lightweight pack onto his shoulders. "I might as well take this with me in case he's hurt."

Grace began shouting for Dr. Harriman while Eric pushed off, also calling. The minute he disappeared from sight, Grace fought down the panicky sensation that she was utterly alone. She could still hear his voice, and that helped.

"Dr. Harriman! Where are you?" she shouted, cupping her hands to her mouth and raising her voice to full volume. "It's Grace. Can you answer?"

Pausing to listen for a response, she heard nothing but the rustling of the grasses in the breeze . . . and then Eric's voice, muffled and distant but reassuringly there.

The sensation of being vulnerable and alone grew as Grace continued to call. The grass swayed around her and Grace had the eerie feeling it was closing in on her, growing thicker somehow. *It's all in your head,* she assured herself. *You're only scared and imagining things.*

Grace listened for the comforting sound of Eric's shouts . . . and heard only the rush of wind through the grass. She waited some more, ears perked, but heard no human voice.

Panic snaked its way up her spine, squeezing her with cold fear. Where was he? How would she find him again? She didn't even know how to find her way out of this field. If she had her phone, Tilly would have her position by satellite and would be directing her every step of the way.

She listened again and heard the rustle of grass being pushed aside, reeds being broken; someone was coming through. It was more than one person.

Eric had found Dr. Harriman!

The reeds parted and two Global-1 police officers stepped through, dressed in their black uniforms. "Grace Morrow?"

This didn't make sense. How had they located her?

"Yes. Have you found my family?"

The officers exchanged darting glances and Grace saw that they didn't understand. "Yes," the taller of the two officers answered. "You need to come with us."

Grace took a step back. Every instinct said he was lying.

Before the decision had even fully formed in her mind, Grace turned into the tall reeds and ran. The underbrush caught on her clothing and the reeds scratched and obstructed her path but she pushed through.

"Stop! Stop where you are!" an officer commanded but she didn't hesitate.

A gunshot rang out and the shock of it dropped Grace to her knees but she kept going, clawing her way through the thorny undergrowth, moving with the desperation of a hunted animal.

From somewhere, a loud beeping sounded. "This way! This way!" the second officer called to the first.

"Grace!" Eric pushed his way through and dropped to his knees beside her. He pulled a sandwich-sized silver packet from his backpack and rapidly unfolded it to ten times its original size. "Get down," he insisted as he pushed Grace flat to the ground with one hand and tossed the silver sheet over her with the other. He lay down beside her, his arms draped over her upper back.

"I've lost the signal." The officers were no more than ten yards away.

"How could that be?" the other officer questioned.

The thunderous pounding of Grace's heart had to be audible — she couldn't believe it wasn't — but the officers began moving off in the opposite direction. "She was right around here when the signal stopped," she heard one of them say, but his voice was receding rather than coming closer.

The sun began beating on the sheet and Grace's skin became moist with sweat. She raised her head. Eric gently but firmly pressed it down again. It seemed to her that she lay there for a long time, steaming under the metallic sheet, frightened to even breathe, pressing her chest into the ground, hoping to quiet the sound of her drumming heartbeat.

Finally, Eric tapped her shoulder blade. "They're gone."

Grace rose on her elbows and began to pull off the sheet. Eric pulled it back over her head. "Keep that on or they'll be back," he warned. "They've got you satellite tracked."

"I don't understand. What's going on?"

"The sheet is blocking the signal. That's why you can't take it off."

"But why would anyone want to track me in the first place? You guys keep talking about a prophecy. Would you please tell me about it?"

"It's time you tell her, Eric." Grace peeked from under the sheet in the direction where a woman's voice had come from, just to Eric's right.

A tall woman of Native American descent stood before her, seemingly appearing out of nowhere. She was a striking woman in her forties, dressed in jeans, boots, and a denim vest. Beaded and turquoise bracelets adorned both of her arms. Her straight black hair was braided down her back. Grace was sure she'd seen this woman somewhere before. But where? Was she on TV, in the movies?

"Eutonah!" Grace breathed as the realization hit her. This was the well-known bar code tattoo resistance fighter, the famed mystic. "You're out of jail," Grace noted. She remembered reading about how, despite all the revelations regarding the bar code tattoo, Eutonah was still being held in jail for her activism against the tattoo.

"She's still in jail," Eric said. "But my mother's spirit is able to travel."

"Your mother?" Grace echoed, surprised.

As Eric nodded, Grace studied Eutonah more keenly and realized that there was something wavering and insubstantial about her presence. It reminded her of the holographic climbing walls. She thought of the holographic FACE-TO-FACE function on her phone. But this was no phoned-in hologram.

"I'll show you to a safe place," Eutonah said. "There we can talk more easily." She turned and spoke directly to Grace. "The time has come for you to understand that we have all been waiting for you. Before it's too late, I must tell you of The Bar Code Prophecy."

TWELVE

The red line subway was becoming increasingly crowded with morning commuters riding the underground rail between downtown Los Angeles and North Hollywood. "You can take that thing off now," Eric told Grace as they entered the subway car.

Grace peeked out from the sheet that she had been holding over her head and shoulders and began to fold it. "I don't understand why I need this," she said.

Eric pointed up. "Satellites. But they can't find you underground."

"I still don't get it," Grace insisted.

Finding no available seat, they stood among the other standing commuters. Grace searched the subway platform for Eutonah, who had left them, saying she'd be back shortly.

"What do you mean about satellites?" Grace asked.

But Eric's focus was on a young man with very dark skin dressed in a gray hooded sweatshirt and baggy jeans. "Hang on a minute," he said to Grace as he left her to weave through the crowd toward the young man. "I'll be right back."

Puzzled, Grace watched as Eric leaned close and whispered something to the hooded man before heading back in her direction.

"Who is that?" Grace asked once Eric had returned.

"Who is who?"

"That guy you just spoke to."

"I didn't speak to anyone."

Grace shot him a look of exasperation and Eric grinned. "I'm just messing with you," he admitted. He bent his head and leaned in close, speaking in the faintest whisper. "He's a Postman. He'll find Kayla and the others. Tell them we're safe."

"How did you know what he was?" Grace whispered back in surprise.

Eric only put his index finger to his lips. "Tell you later."

The subway rushed along its underground track and Grace wished she had some idea where they were headed. She had so many questions and not nearly enough answers. "Why didn't you tell me your mother is Eutonah?" she said.

"You never asked," Eric joked, but then grew serious. "As you know, my mother is still in jail, despite all the people calling for her release. When she became active in the resistance to the bar code tattoo, I went to live with my uncle, Russell Chaca. People call him Chief Russell. My dad died years ago. We all figured it would be better if everyone didn't realize I was Eutonah's son. It would keep me safer."

"I guess that means you have Cherokee background. I always heard you were Hopi."

"Dad's Hopi and some Irish. Mom's Cherokee. They met at Dartmouth."

"Tell me about the prophecy," Grace whispered.

"Not here," Eric replied softly.

They rode for several stops until Eric indicated with a nod

that they should get off. The platform at their stop was empty and Grace followed Eric to the end. "What are you doing?" she gasped as Eric leaped off the end, rolling to a standing stop on the dirt ground with exceptional agility.

"Your turn," he said, smiling up at her.

He thinks I can't, Grace realized, interpreting the bravado in his grin as a challenge. Could she? Grace wasn't certain. She was used to landing on gym mats, not hard dirt. And she would be falling to a lower level.

Without further consideration, Grace ran a few steps before launching into a forward flip. When she planted her landing, her right ankle caved slightly from the uneven rocky dirt under her feet. Still, she was standing.

"Final level!" Eric praised her. "I told them you were going to be great at this."

"Great at what?" Grace asked, working hard not to beam with self-satisfied pride.

"You'll see. I'll show you later." Eric beckoned for her to follow him for several yards deeper into the tunnel.

"The door is right there." Eutonah's voice came from behind Grace.

"How did you — ?" Grace cut herself short. The mysterious Eutonah could be anywhere, apparently.

Eric used a key to unlock a room no larger than a walk-in closet. When they were inside, he turned on a single bulb that glared from the ceiling and relocked the door. Eutonah opened a metal case in the corner and lifted out a helmet. Grace had never seen anything like it. It had a small keyboard and miniature computer screen in the front and wire wrapped around.

"A virtual reality helmet," Eutonah explained. She took a cord from the box and plugged the middle of it into the helmet's keyboard so that a cord of equal length extended from either side. "This extender allows all three of us to use it at once."

"Use it how?" Grace asked nervously, noticing that each end of the cord contained an elastic loop.

"Don't be frightened; there is no danger in this," Eutonah assured Grace as she punched numbers into the keyboard. Eutonah then settled on the ground in a cross-legged sitting position. Eric sat on her left and indicated with a gesture that Grace should be seated on Eutonah's right side. Grace followed Eric's example as he slipped the end of one half of the cord around his wrist and she did the same with the opposite end.

"Close your eyes and hold my hand," Eutonah instructed them. "You're going to feel like you have traveled, but you will really be here the whole time."

"Can't you do that already without this device?" Grace questioned.

"I'm able to travel," Eutonah agreed, "but neither of you can. At least not yet."

So many questions played on the tip of Grace's tongue, but before she could voice any of them, a tingling sensation overtook every inch of her skin. It went deeper into her body until she felt that her bones were vibrating and her skull itself quivered with an unsettling buzz.

Grace was about to cry out, to demand that Eutonah shut the helmet down, when all the shaking abruptly stopped.

She was no longer in the dingy subway closet but stood on an immense flat rock. A vivid sky pressed down on a vast expanse of orange-brown desert with areas of green shrubbery. Jagged mountains towered in the distance. It surprised her that although she was alone, she felt no fear. There was something strangely soothing in the utter silence of this majestic place.

"We are a thousand feet above sea level," Eutonah said.

Grace turned to find Eutonah and Eric behind her. "We are on sacred Hopi land," Eutonah continued. "The Hopi believe that this is the center of the universe."

This wasn't hard for Grace to accept. She could feel the power of the place coursing into her, energizing her spine, her limbs, even her mind. Never before had she experienced such a calm and centered sensation of complete well-being.

"This is Spider Rock, the great place of vision for the many. We're in Navajo territory, which rings the Hopi lands," Eutonah told them.

Grace felt as if she could touch the turquoise sky. Below her was an expanse of red rock desert ringed with boulders and mesas.

"Five years ago the leaders of many Native American nations met here for a secret tribunal," Eutonah went on. "I was among the delegation representing the Cherokee Nation. We came to discuss nothing less important than the future of this planet. The delegates from each tribe gathered their end-of-days prophecies to see what we could learn about what is to come."

"What did you conclude?" Eric asked.

"We found a lot of overlap in the different myths and predictions, and the Hopi seemed to have the most well-developed prophecies. Many of the events predicted — the coming of the white man, the loss of our lands, and the oil spill devastation back in 2010 — have come to pass already."

"Does that mean the end of the world is near?" Grace asked.

"It might be; we're not sure. So many of the prophecies have come to pass. The Hopi believe there will be great destruction on Earth, but that they will be carried from the destroyed Earth on wingless flying ships."

"What will happen to everyone else?" Grace asked.

"The Hopi have nine prophecies, all of which have been fulfilled. A tenth prophecy has been discovered. Very few have ever seen it."

"What does it say?" Eric asked.

"We call it The Bar Code Prophecy."

Grace viewed the bar code tattoo on her wrist. "This bar code?"

"Yes," Eutonah confirmed with a nod. "We call it that because we believe that the lines of destruction that the tenth Hopi prophecy refers to are the lines of the bar code tattoo."

"Why would you think that?" Eric inquired, his brows knit in concerned concentration.

Eutonah headed to the edge of the rock mesa on which they stood and laid on her stomach, beckoning for Grace and Eric to do the same. "See that opening cut in the mountain?" Eutonah said, pointing straight down. "Can you get down to it, Eric?"

"Sure I can," Eric answered confidently.

If anyone could, it was Eric — but a slip would be certain death. They should return with climbing line. Before Grace was able to express her concern, Eric was flat against the side of the mesa. She held her breath, not wanting to disturb his concentration in any way.

With cautious but deliberate movements, Eric made his way toward the opening in the mesa wall, sometimes clinging by his fingertips. Grace was torn between fascination and her desire to look away. A sidelong glance at Eutonah revealed that the woman's face had become a stone mask, reflecting nothing but absorption in Eric's progress.

When Grace dared to look at Eric again, he was withdrawing a stone tablet of about twelve by eight inches from the opening. He tucked it into the belted waist of his jeans and began his ascent.

Only when his hand appeared above the edge of the mesa did Grace feel it was safe for her to move. Scrambling to the edge, she clutched his wrist to assist his return. Before rising, he passed the stone tablet up and she took it from him with her free hand. Eutonah laid on her stomach and helped pull Eric up and over to safety.

"Thanks," he said, lying on his back beside Grace and his mother.

"Here's why we think there is a tenth prophecy," Eutonah revealed, sitting with the tablet on her knee. Leaning in close to Eutonah, Grace saw a series of pictographs, straight lines, and stick figures. Below these were writings in English, as if someone had interpreted the meaning of the pictographs. Eutonah began to read the engraved writing:

Our brother shall return. He will bring with him the innocent daughter fathered by the master of destruction. The heavenly bodies will know her every move by the lines of destruction the father has carved on her arm. She will flee him but the master's warriors will not stop until they pull the heavenly bodies to the earth and then . . .

The tingling that had rung in Grace's skull returned full force. Her hands flew to her head and she squeezed her eyes shut. Eutonah's hand encircled Grace's wrist and she was traveling once more.

THIRTEEN

When Grace reopened her eyes, she was once again in the dank, harshly lit subway storage closet. Eutonah and Eric were with her. "The time ran out," Eutonah explained. "The helmet runs on a timer for our own protection."

"Do you know the rest of the prophecy?" Grace asked.

"What you heard is all anyone knows," Eutonah told them. "During the meeting of chieftains, we used the prophecies to lead us to the stone tablet hidden in the mesa wall. Several of the elders interpreted the pictographs, but the tablet was broken. Somewhere there is a missing piece."

"What do the elders think it means?" Eric asked.

"You are too young to remember this, but back in the year 2012, many people believed that the Mayan calendar had predicted the end of the world would arrive in December of that year," Eutonah said.

"Obviously it didn't," Eric pointed out.

"The date seemed to come and go without event, but there are many of us who believe it was the beginning of the end," Eutonah countered. "It was the year Jonathan Harriman invented the bar code tattoo and Global-1 first launched it in Asia. It took only another thirteen years for the tattoo to spread through Africa and then Europe before it got to America in 2025."

"So you're saying the Mayan prophecy did come to pass, after all?" Grace said.

"Yes. It just happened very quietly," Eutonah said with a nod. "But there are those among the chieftains who believe that we are in the final stages of the prophecy."

"What's supposed to happen?" Eric asked

"No one knows, but much of what happens in the end will be up to the two of you."

"Us?!" Grace cried.

"We think Eric is the brother mentioned in the prophecies," Eutonah replied. "He combines the blood of two great Indian nations. His father was descended from a line of Hopi chieftains. On my side he is descended from powerful Cherokee shamans, spiritual men and women with highly developed gifts."

"And me because my biological father is Jonathan Harriman?" Grace deducted. "Is he really the Master of Destruction?"

"It might not ever have been his intention to harm anyone," Eutonah allowed, "but the thing he invented and the company that has grown rich and so powerful because of his invention makes him an excellent candidate for the title."

"What about the heavenly bodies falling from the skies?" Eric asked.

"We don't know," Eutonah admitted. "But we do know this: The Hopi believe that the land we were just now on is the center of the universe, and Global-1 is strip-mining it for minerals. Every day they use gallons and gallons of precious water to make a slurry of liquid chemicals and water because it's the least expensive way to transport the minerals."

Grace realized Eutonah's meaning. "The balance of the world is being upset."

"Of the *universe*," Eric amended.

"The moon affects the tides; who's to say that the mineral content of the Earth doesn't affect things floating in space?" Eutonah said. "If the center of the universe is destroyed by the greed of Global-1, who knows what could happen?"

Grace suddenly felt that she couldn't catch her breath. This was all too much. "This is crazy," she said, panic rising in her voice. "I don't believe in prophecies. And even if it's all true, what does it have to do with me?"

"You're the daughter the prophecy talks about," Eutonah replied.

"I'm not!" Grace refused to believe it. "I'm Grace Morrow and I have a family that is missing. I have no right to be fooling around with all of this right now. I need to be looking for them."

"Your best hope of finding them is with us," Eric insisted as he laid his hand reassuringly on her arm.

"I don't believe you!" Grace cried, pulling away from his touch. "You're all involved in this bar code tattoo resistance and that's all you want me for." She grabbed the keys Eutonah had placed on the virtual reality helmet case and opened the door. "I'm sorry, but I can't help you. I have to find my family."

The moment Grace stepped out, she almost collided with a subway car zooming down the track. It plastered her to the side of the wall, throwing dirt and debris in her face.

As soon as it had passed, she ran down the track and was able to pull herself up onto the platform at the end of the subway car and let herself inside. She slipped into a seat by the back car, panting heavily from the effort.

Commuters slipped wary sidelong glances at Grace, and she realized how disreputable she must look, covered in dirt from the passing train and with her hair knotted and windswept from her parachute jump. Her stomach grumbled loudly, reminding her that all she'd eaten since the day before was a granola bar that she'd hastily bought on the way to the subway station.

A dirty, disheveled man bearing a sign entered the train. It read: THE END IS NEAR. People moved away from him, seeming unconcerned with anything other than his pungent body odor.

"Brothers and sisters," the man addressed the crowd in a loud voice as the subway train left the station. "You must understand that we have reached the last days of this evil, corrupt world. Prepare to breathe your last."

Withdrawing a harmonica from his pocket, the dirty prophet began to play an old song that Grace recognized; in her head she sang the verses, which were about it being the end of the world as she knew it. When he was done, he leaned in close to each commuter, asking that they donate money in repayment for his song. The train was pulling into the next station when he reached Grace. She hoped to escape him but he blocked her path before she could fully rise from her seat. He leaned in so close that their cheeks touched. She recoiled from his awful odor.

"I'm a Postman," he whispered. "I know where your family is. Follow me out at this stop, but not too closely."

The subway doors opened, and before Grace could decide if she should trust him, he was moving toward the exit.

In a second she would lose sight of him altogether.

Grace began moving, uncertain if it was the right thing to do. But what choice did she have? If she didn't act on this, she was at a dead end. Commuters clustered in the doorway, forcing Grace to push her way through.

The subway doors whooshed shut, catching the hem of her shirt. The train began to pull forward. Frightened that she would be dragged along, Grace pulled at the hem with all her strength. The hem tore and ripped the bottom half of the garment, tearing off as the train picked up speed.

Grace searched in every direction for the man who had claimed to be a Postman, and spied him at the top of the station stairs. With a spring, she rushed up the steps, weaving past departing commuters, ignoring their curses and complaints as she pushed past them. When she reached the top, the Postman had moved down the block and was pretending to loiter at a newsstand.

As she approached, their eyes met for just a flicker before he once again moved ahead. Confident now that he would wait for her, Grace relaxed enough to allow herself to take a good look at her guide. From the strength and agility of his movement, she realized that he was younger than he had appeared at first, maybe in his mid-twenties. In fact, not only did he move with the poise and speed of a young person, he traveled with exceptional ease, rolling easily over a garbage can that had fallen in his path and navigating around a dog walker with five dogs without breaking the fluidity of his movement.

Grace was impressed and recalled the catlike ease with which Eric had jumped into a rolling stand when he'd leaped from the subway platform.

The Postman crossed a busy street into a park, and Grace was delayed at the red light. Once she'd crossed, it took her an anxious moment before she saw him lying on the grass at the other end of the park's diagonal path. She was hurrying in his direction when a shadow crossed her path. Stopping short, Grace faced two black-uniformed Global-1 officers.

"Grace Morrow, you must come with us."

"Have you found my family?" Grace asked hopefully.

"Just come with us, please."

"How did you find me?" Grace wondered aloud. Was it really true that without the silver sheet they could track her every movement?

Over the officer's shoulder, Grace spied the Postman shuffling anxiously. Who knew where her family was, the Postman or Global-1? Who should she trust?

"We were sent to get you," the Global-1 officer said.

"But how did you know where I was?" Grace repeated, backing away.

"We'll take you to your family," the officer said.

When the Postman had said the same thing, she'd followed him. Why did she want to run from these Global-1 officers now? "Where are we going?" she asked them, continuing to back up.

"If you don't cooperate, we'll be forced to arrest you."

"Arrest me for what?" Grace asked.

The officer reached for her and Grace took off running. She ran with every inch of strength and lung power in her, racing toward the Postman but not seeing him. The officers chased, but were obstructed by a line of small children on a camp trip.

Grace sped down the city street, careening around a corner only to be met by a parked Global-1 squad car. As the officers from the car approached, she ducked through traffic, keeping low and ran down the closest side street on the other side. When she reached the end, two more Global-1 officers appeared.

Running off to her right, they didn't seem to be trying that hard to catch her. It was as though they were so certain she couldn't escape that they were taking their time, tightening their grip on her gradually. The idea demoralized her, made her feel she was already caught in their trap.

Grace panted as she turned into an alley. Another squad car cruised to a stop out on the street and Grace turned to see she was trapped by a brick building at the end of the alley. No officers yet, but she was sure they were coming.

"On belay." Grace looked up to the direction of the voice and saw Eric looking down at her from the rooftop. He was about two stories high and he'd thrown down a rope that had a loop tied to the end. "But make it fast," he added as she stepped into the loop.

Reaching up, Grace gripped the mortar that held the bricks and began to climb. When she was nearly to the top, a piece of brick crumbled beneath her hand and she lost hold. In her surprise, she slipped and swung out from the building.

"Got ya," Eric assured her from above. "You're almost here. Refocus and keep coming up."

Grace found her holds once more and continued to the top. Eric helped hoist her over the ledge while he gazed anxiously up at the sky and then down below.

"They've lost us?" Grace suggested hopefully.

"They can always find you," Eric said. "For the rest of your life, they're always going to be able to find you." He held a device the size of a cell phone over her and it began to buzz. "But for now, we're jamming their signal." He did a quick comic dance around her singing as he went, "We be jammin'. We be jammin'." Then he stopped and grabbed her arm. "Now let's get out of here."

FOURTEEN

"We suspected it, but now we're almost certain," Kayla said. She sat on the hood of a car parked in the same underground garage that Grace had been in the day before. Grace was standing beside Eric and Mfumbe, all of them leaning against a parked tractor trailer.

"We're pretty sure you've been nano-chipped," Kayla went on. "We have information that everyone who received the bar code tattoo in the last three months was injected with a microscopic tracking chip. It's as if they put a molecular-sized cell phone inside you and it's constantly pinging."

"Pinging?" Grace questioned.

"Sending signals to a tracking satellite," Mfumbe clarified.

"Global-1 has been working on this idea for a while. My mother, who was a maternity nurse, saw them actually inserting chips into the feet of infants," Kayla continued. "We included this in the information we sent to Ambrose Young, and he exposed it in the Senate investigation. Global-1 admitted it and claimed it was simply an anti-kidnapping measure. Global-1 was ordered to shut it down."

"So now they're trying it another way," Mfumbe said.

"I want it out of me!" Grace cried. The idea that something had been put in her body without her permission or knowledge was such a violation. The notion that it was a tracking device made her feel like an animal caught in a net. "Do you mean that Global-1 is following the movements of everyone my age?"

"Not everyone," Kayla replied. "They're not interested in locating everyone. But they *can* locate anyone who is your age just by punching in satellite coordinates that they took when you were tattooed."

"You're Jonathan Harriman's daughter. Most likely they want to use you to get to him," Mfumbe said.

"He doesn't care about me," Grace argued. "I barely know him."

"He might care more than you think," Kayla said. "My guess is that they want something from him and he's not cooperating. They want you as a bargaining tool."

"And it's possible they know about the prophecy," Eric pointed out.

"Maybe," Kayla said. "But maybe not."

"And that's why they went after my family? As a bargaining tool, too?" Grace asked.

"We think so," Mfumbe replied. "When they didn't get you at your house, they took your family knowing you would come to the police looking for them. Besides that, your adoptive parents might know more about the Global-1 program than they want revealed."

Again, Grace clung to the hope that they'd gotten away. But it seemed less and less likely.

"You know what? I don't care about any of this. I only want to find my family."

"We're going to find them," Eric told her. "You and me together."

"How can you find them?" Grace challenged.

"Finding people is what I do. I'm a Postman. And I'm going to train you to be a Postman, too. I've been watching you. You've got the stuff to do it. Becoming a Postman is going to give you the skills to find anyone you want, including your family."

Eric unlocked the back door of the climbing center. "The reason we get to use this place is because the owner is a Postman. He encourages us to train here."

"Are we going to do more climbing?" Grace asked.

"Maybe later. Today I'm going to start your training as a free runner."

"A what?"

"It's kind of like being an urban ninja; you move through a city landscape with the fluidity of water flowing through rocks, with complete ease and total efficiency."

"The Postman I followed the other day moved like that," Grace recalled.

"He was just playing," Eric said. "You should see him when he's trying."

"How do you know?"

"I told him where to find you, and I was trailing you," Eric revealed. "How do you think I just happened to pop up on that rooftop?"

"Then he doesn't know where my family is?" Grace asked, disappointed.

"I don't know if he knows. Did he say he did?"

Grace nodded. "The Global-1 cops said they knew, too. Is everyone lying to me?"

"The cops probably were," Eric concluded. "But the Postman might really know where they are. Your family might be trying to send you a message. If the message was meant only for you, he wouldn't tell me no matter how much he trusted me. It's in the Postman's code, a way of insuring the privacy of other people's messages."

He reached into his backpack and pulled out a silver bolero vest. "Put this on," he said, handing it to her. "Allyson made it for you. It should shield you from the tracking devices."

Eric took the jamming device from his backpack. "I'm setting this up because that vest isn't going to do the entire job," he told her. "Every time that tracker chip circulates out from under that vest, they can find you. Ideally you should be covered from head to toe."

"How hot and uncomfortable!" Grace remarked.

"I know. Everyone is going to start dressing like medieval knights in armor. It will be coming back in fashion," Eric joked.

"It'll be kind of hard to move around."

"I know. We'll all be living underground wearing armor. Not much fun. I kind of like sunlight."

"But people who have no reason to hide won't have to worry," Grace pointed out.

"Yeah, only dangerous criminals like you will have to go underground."

"But I'm not —"

"That's my point. Anyone who gets in Global-1's way can

be picked up and eliminated." Eric snapped his fingers. "Easy as that."

Grace put on the vest as Eric led her down steps and into a very large basement gym furnished with ropes, immense foam cubes, and pits of foam blocks, trapeze swings, an uneven parallel bar and a balance beam. "Ever take gymnastics?" he asked.

"I took classes as a kid and I'm on the team in school. I was supposed to be captain of the team this coming year."

"I thought so. You move like a gymnast."

"I'm tall though. All the really good gymnasts are on the shorter side."

"I bet the balance beam is your best piece," Eric said.

"It is," Grace confirmed. "How did you know?"

"The way you move. Grace is a good name for you."

Eric smiled and seemed to gaze straight inside her. She was suddenly certain he felt something for her, a feeling other than friendship. He was close enough to kiss her and Grace thought he was about to. She wanted him to.

"I'm going to show you a training hologram," Eric said instead.

"Final level," Grace replied, hoping he couldn't tell what she'd been thinking.

Eric went to the wall and clicked a button. Multicolored particles tingled in the air and formed into the shape of the gray-hooded young Postman Eric had spoken to in the subway.

"He's not actually here, of course," Eric explained. "But he made the video and is the model for the hologram. His name is Javaun."

The hologram of Javaun began running very fast around

the gym. Grace was amazed as he ran up the side of a padded wall, nearly to the ceiling, and then back down again. Launching himself over the pit of foam blocks, he spun in the air and rolled to a standing stop on the other side and kept moving to the parallel bars, which he spun on, changing hands several times before shooting over to the balance beam, executing a backward walk-over, and spinning to the floor.

"Wow," Grace breathed, genuinely awed.

"That's just a training session. Wait until you see it in real life. People think the Postmen have gone away, but we haven't. There's more need for us now than ever. In fact, we've stepped up our game by adding free running."

"Can you do all that?" Grace asked.

"Yep," Eric said with a nod. "And soon you'll be able to, as well."

"I don't think so." Grace couldn't imagine it.

"You will, because I'm going to teach you and I'm one of the best teachers around," Eric insisted.

"Modest, too," Grace teased.

"No reason for modesty at this juncture. It is what it is," Eric said.

For the next five hours, Eric and Grace went outside where Grace experienced the most grueling training of her life. Despite her years of experience with gymnastics, she felt like a beginner.

"Grab hold! Pretend you're a bug on a wall!" he instructed her.

"You can run faster than that! Race up that wall before gravity knows you're there," he shouted.

"Roll! Roll! And on your feet!"

At the end of the training session, Grace felt sweaty and broken. "Not bad for the first session. Tomorrow we'll try some basic urban free," Eric said.

"How long have you been a Postman?" Grace asked Eric as they returned to the basement, safely underground.

"Just for the last year," Eric replied. "I love it. It tests your body and your mind to the max. Plus, I'm helping people to not have their every communication monitored by Global-1. That makes me feel good."

"In what ways does it test your mind?" Grace wanted to know. The ways in which it tested the body were obvious.

"You have to look for the links between people, as well as between places," Eric replied. "Ever hear of six degrees of separation?"

"No."

"It's the idea that everyone in the world is connected to everyone else in six moves. Say I have to get a note to a guy in Brooklyn, New York. I search him on the Internet, and for most people there is a ton of info there. Sometimes I can find the address right online. In that case I just find a Postman heading that way and pass on the message. If I can't, I start looking for people with the same last name, people who work in the same business, have similar interests, who went to the same school, and on and on. Lots of the time you wind up finding the friend of a friend of a friend who worked with a guy who knows the person's sister. The Postman's goal is to do it in no more than six moves."

"It doesn't sound easy," Grace remarked. "How do you know which Postman to contact?"

"You hear things and talk to people. After a while, you'll get to know. I'll help you," Eric assured her.

"Do the Postmen all know each other?"

"Yeah, but it takes a while," Eric replied. "It's better if we know Postmen to hand messages off to, but there's no central directory or anything. You just have to get to know people."

"What about the Postman who said he knew where my family was? Do you know him?"

"That guy who poses as a subway nut? His name is Darrell. Javaun is a friend of his. They work the subway a lot. I'll find him for you."

"Do you think you could?"

"Sure. I'll ask him what he knows," Eric assured her. "Grace, you're going to be good at this. I think you'll like it, too."

Grace was excited to try being a Postman, but it still sounded daunting to her. The long hours of training had taxed her to her limit and she couldn't quite imagine doing it again in the morning. "Can I rest now?" she asked.

"Find a piece of foam and settle in," Eric told her.

Dropping into a pit of foam blocks, Grace piled some blocks under her head and stretched out. She was aware of every muscle of her body because each one felt hot and stretched to its limit; each joint ached.

Eric piled three mats down and lay on his stomach. "Are you still mad at me, Grace?"

"I don't mind working hard," she answered. "I want to learn it."

"Not about that. I know you're not mad about that," Eric

said. "But you were angry when you learned I was the one assigned to follow you."

This wasn't her instructor talking. Or a Postman. Or a Decode operative. Suddenly, Eric was a guy again — the guy who went to her high school. The guy she'd liked.

The truth was, Grace wasn't mad anymore. Just sad. Still.

"I thought we were really . . . friends," she said, ready to leave it at that.

"We've become friends. I really like you, Grace. I think you're smart and brave."

"Thanks."

"And pretty . . . beautiful, really."

Grace drew in a long, slow breath. *Beautiful.* He thought she was *beautiful.* She had never thought of herself that way but it was enough that he did.

"I mean it, Grace. I'm not just giving you a line. Being assigned to follow you was like a gift. It's been the best assignment I've ever had."

"Thanks, Eric . . . for saying all that. It means a lot for me to know you're not just spending time with me because you have no choice."

"I hope you'll always spend time with me," Eric said softly. "I don't like the idea of being separated from you."

His words made Grace take a short, quick breath of surprised delight. Did he mean that? "Me neither," she replied, suddenly certain that she meant it. Being with Eric was so natural. His confidence made her feel that everything could be managed and would come out all right in the end. Even with so many things going so wrong.

Eric yawned widely as he stretched. "We should sleep. Tomorrow will be just as hard as today."

"Can't wait," Grace replied without a trace of sarcasm. "Good night," she added, drifting off to sleep with a smile lingering on her lips.

In the morning, Eric gently shook her awake and handed her a carton of orange juice and a buttered roll. Brushing hair from her eyes, she sat up and drank. "Thanks."

"Today we're going to start you free running outside," Eric said. "You'll have to wear the jacket."

"What's it like outside?"

"Not bad," he answered, "but there's a strange light in the sky. I'm not sure how to describe it. It's almost as if the sun is extra bright."

Pasadena Sun

Pasadena, California — July 14, 2026

Solar Flares Disrupt Worldwide Communications

A report today from the U.S. National Oceanic and Atmospheric Administration (NOAA) claims that vastly increased solar activity in the sun's corona has created a sudden brightness in the sky and has disrupted many communication venues that rely on satellite signals. Lead scientist Heather Mitchell explains that "streams of high energy particles known as solar wind events or coronal mass ejection impact the Earth's magnetosphere and represent hazards to spacecraft and satellites."

NOAA claims that its scientists did not anticipate this development to happen for many hundreds of years. "This is the most unprecedented solar activity we have ever observed in all the years we have been studying solar activity," Mitchell noted.

When asked what might be causing this, Mitchell replied that NASA scientists are divided in their opinion. "Some are of the mind that this is simply a solar pattern much like what the Earth goes through with fluctuations in its temperature. Others believe that there is some change in the overall atmosphere that is causing this. Since Earth is the only inhabited planet, to our knowledge, there are those who think changes here on Earth might be prompting these solar irregularities." NASA has even called in a Native American shaman from the Iroquois Nation who told reporters, "The native people from across the continent are meeting to discuss this issue. The Earth is not in balance. As in a human body, when one of the parts is ill, the other parts are affected. So it is with the universe."

PART THREE

I'm still trying to make my mind up
Am I free or am I tied up?

— "Animal"
Song written by Henrik Nils Jonback,
Pontus Johan Winnberg, Andrew Wyatt
Blakemore, and Christian Lars Karlsson

FIFTEEN

Kayla leaned against one of the cars parked in the garage and handed Grace a shopping bag. "Some presents for your big day," she said with a grin. Today would be Grace's first run as a Postman.

When Grace pulled the black hip-length jacket from the bag, the silver lining crinkled gently. "Reach in the pocket," Kayla added.

When she reached in, Grace found a metal box resembling one of the larger old-style cell phones. It was the same kind of signal jammer Eric had used that day on the roof.

"Global-1 is still searching for you," Kayla said. "They've got to be. And that means they are still scanning the area, just waiting for your signal to beep onto their screens."

"But why?"

"They're thinking that they can use you to find Dr. Harriman," Kayla replied.

"How do you know that?"

"We *don't* know it for sure," Kayla admitted. "They might have Harriman already. But they might not, and we don't want to risk it."

"What do you think they want him for?"

Kayla shrugged and shook her head. "He's their genius. Maybe he wants out. Maybe he's threatening to go public and tell all he knows about all their dirty dealings."

"What do you think would happen if he did that?" Grace asked.

Kayla's face grew somber as she hopped up onto the car's hood and sat cross-legged there a moment before answering. "I don't know, Grace. It's possible that nothing would happen. Global-1 already has their man in the White House. Who knows how many leaders they control in other countries? Ambrose Young is one of our most powerful public figures, and he can't bring them down."

"So why do you keep fighting them?"

Again, Kayla took a while before answering, as though she were asking herself the same question and digging deep for the truth. Grace knew Kayla's story — all the running, hiding; all the lies that had been told about her; all the personal loss she'd suffered. What could possibly keep her going?

"I fight because I'm alive and every living thing longs to be free," Kayla said, finally. "I feel as if I've had a net thrown over me by Global-1. We all do what Global-1 wants us to do, live the way they say, believe what their commercials and TV news want us to believe. It's set up so that they can get richer and greedier and more powerful by the day. And all the while they destroy the planet we inhabit and make our lives smaller. But I know there's more mystery, happiness, and meaning in life than what they're offering. In my heart I feel the world can be better than what it is. We all believe it, and Eutonah helped us see it."

"Was that when you studied with her in the Adirondack Mountains?" Grace knew Kayla and Mfumbe had studied spirituality and even telepathy with Eutonah's group before Global-1 had raided them, jailing Eutonah.

Kayla's face softened and she smiled gently. "Eutonah is my hero. When I think of her, I become sure there is more to a person than just being a product branded with a bar code. I know it because she's so much more."

"But Global-1 is so huge and powerful," Grace said.

"I know," Kayla agreed, sliding off the hood of the car and seeming to regain her all-business attitude. "So we'll fight them little piece by little piece. Katie and Mfumbe have taken the truck back to one of our outposts in the Great Basin Desert. The caves there are perfect because no radar or satellite signal can penetrate. They're picking up a new batch of tattoo fakes."

"A lot of people are involved in this movement, aren't they?" Grace asked.

"More and more every day," Kayla said. "People are getting fed up. Now let's see how that cloaking jacket fits you."

Grace pulled on the jacket, disliking the feel of the lining and a slight tightness at the shoulders. Sighing with resignation, she dropped the jammer into the pocket. If fighting Global-1 meant wearing a hot, ill-fitting jacket, then that's how it had to be. Besides, this was her best bet for finding her family and staying out of Global-1's clutches.

"Looking good, Grace!" Allyson walked toward them from the back of the garage. "That jacket makes you look very anonymous and indistinct. You might want to tie your hair back, too, for a totally nondescript effect. Postmen aim to blend in with the scenery."

Jack was beside her and he held a manila envelope. "In here is your first assignment. It shouldn't be that difficult, but it's really important. We thought it would be a good way to start you out because the guy we want you to find is right here in the city. His name is Harry Clemente and he works for the people who fund the swing-lo production. We're asking for additional funding to add stealth technology to make it invisible to radar and satellite tracking."

"We also want to get into mass production," Allyson added. "We think we're ready."

"Even after the last one fell apart?" Kayla questioned skeptically.

"Yeah, but now I know how high it can go — or can't go," Jack said. "Don't worry. I'll test the next one myself. I'd like to get out to the desert again and try it unobstructed by buildings." Jack looked to Kayla and smiled. "Remember when we were out in the desert, zipping around in that ratty first model?"

"I couldn't believe I was really in a spaceship," Kayla told everyone. "It didn't seem real."

"But now you're used to it, aren't you?" Allyson said.

"I am. It's true," Kayla agreed.

Jack handed Grace the envelope and she saw there was no address. "Where do I go?" she asked.

"You're a Postman now. You've got to find him. Sometimes I see him in Katz's Diner in downtown Hollywood. Start there. There's a fake tattoo in there. Ask him to put the bar code credits into the bank account encoded there. See if he wants you to wait for an answer."

"Is Eric going with me?"

"No. He's on his own run this morning. It's all yours."

Grace took the subway toward downtown Los Angeles, feeling self-conscious in her foil lined jacket. Every time she moved she was acutely aware of the soft crinkling of the material. Besides that, it was brutally hot out; the news reported over one hundred Fahrenheit, and to be in a jacket made her feel conspicuous in addition to being overheated. At least the subway was air-conditioned.

She'd found the address of Katz's Diner and was headed for it. Surely someone there would know of Harry Clemente. The assignment seemed incredibly simple, requiring no free-running and not much brain power, either. Grace was glad for her first assignment to be a no-brainer.

Katz's Diner was only half full when Grace sat at the counter and ordered scrambled eggs and toast. "Do you know a man named Harry Clemente?" she asked the waitress.

The waitress smiled at her. "Postman?" she inquired in the barest of whispers.

Grace shook her head in reply. Eric had instructed her never to admit to being a Postman. It might be a trap. Being a Postman was illegal, and rewards were offered to anyone who turned one in to authorities. "No. He's my uncle and I need to find him."

"Well, your *Aunt* Stephanie just walked in," the waitress said, and from her ironic tone, Grace knew she'd failed to convince the woman. She tilted her head toward a tall blond woman of about forty.

"Thanks," Grace said. Normally she would have presented her arm so the waitress could run her handheld scanner over it for payment. But she remembered that Eric had told her not to buy anything along the way. It was another way Global-1 could find her. Unfortunately she hadn't remembered this until she was halfway through her meal.

The waitress looked at her and then leaned in close. "Postmen eat free here," she whispered.

With a grateful smile and a nod of appreciation, Grace went across the diner and slipped into the booth beside the woman identified as Aunt Stephanie. "Hi. I have a message for Harry Clemente," she said to the surprised looking woman.

"What's it about?" Aunt Stephanie asked, sipping her coffee.

"Private, only for Harry Clemente."

"I'm his wife."

Grace shrugged apologetically.

The woman took a pen from her bag and scribbled an address onto a napkin. "And tell him to pick up a carton of eggs on his way home tonight," she added, sliding the napkin to Grace.

Grace was quickly on her way. She arrived at a building that seemed abandoned and double-checked the address. Had the woman played some kind of joke on her? Grace walked into the alley and craned her neck to see up to the top, searching for some sign that the building was inhabited, but every window was dark. Reluctantly, she stepped into the shadowy front lobby. The address indicated that Harry Clemente was in apartment 1L. There were no apartments on the lobby level. She hit the elevator button only to discover that the buttons were torn out — all but one. Basement level L.

Taking the car down, Grace realized she was sweating heavily in the closed elevator car but was afraid to remove her jacket. When the door slid open, Grace faced a harshly lit room containing only a man in a dusty-looking velvet maroon armchair. He was very fat and balding, and sat there reading the paper.

"Hot enough for you?" he said as Grace stepped out of the elevator.

"Too hot," Grace replied, stepping into the room.

"And this crazy bright sun, huh?" he continued. "What's that about already?"

"Solar flares. I read about it in the newspaper," Grace offered. "I'm looking for Harry Clemente."

"Speaking."

"You're Harry Clemente?" Grace checked.

"Who's asking?"

Grace didn't know how to answer. She'd forgotten if Eric's instruction to never admit to being a Postman applied to when she'd found her subject.

The man and Grace stared at each other awkwardly. "I have a message for Harry Clemente," Grace ventured. "Could I see some proof that you're him?"

"And you are?" the man pressed.

"A friend — with a message."

The man seemed amused. He picked up something metal that had been wedged between his corpulent leg and the side of the chair and pointed it at Grace.

Panicked, Grace turned back toward the elevator. Its doors had closed and she saw no buttons.

The man chortled. "Here's my proof I'm Harry Clemente," the man said, holding the metal piece in the air. The white wall behind him slid open, revealing a large room filled with desks. At each desk, people congregated talking in low, serious whispers. Some read, others wrote. Grace noticed there were no phones or computers.

"Welcome to Decode headquarters," the man said, rising from his chair. "I know who you are. We've been watching you."

SIXTEEN

Grace sat in Decode headquarters, waiting for Harry Clemente to return with a response. Beside her a wiry, dark-haired young man in his twenties lay on the floor poring over a large book of maps. Noticing Grace reading over his shoulder, he glanced up and smiled. "Hi, I'm Nate. You're new here."

"I'm Grace. Yes, this is my first day."

He looked her over. "I'm guessing from that jacket that you're a Postman."

"You're not supposed to be able to guess that."

"You get an eye for it after a while. The jacket is too conspicuously nondescript."

"What?"

"You're trying too hard to blend in. No one is that bland."

"It's also roasting."

"Take it off," Nate advised. "You're deep enough underground." As she removed the jacket, relieved to be free of it, Nate's eyes went to the silver lining. "You're seventeen," he remarked.

"Yeah. How could you tell?"

"You're chipped. Seventeen-year-olds. It's the newest wave of Global-1 evil."

"It's horrible."

Nate's expression became skeptical. "It's creepy but we're all trackable, with or without the nanochip. Our phones send off signals, all our electronics do. That's why we work without them down here, even though we think it's safe. We're not one hundred percent sure, so we don't take chances. The signal jammers we have are nothing compared to the powerful ones Global-1 has. Ours just mess up their satellite signals for a few minutes."

"But they can find me anywhere," Grace said.

"They can see us all. From way high in the air they can locate our whereabouts and then focus down small enough to read our bar codes if we're unlucky enough to have one. Plus, there are surveillance cameras. We've grown so used to them that we don't even notice them anymore. But they're there. Putting that chip in you guys just eliminates *all* the guesswork. They don't even have to bother to look for you. You're broadcasting all the time. You're like a dog in one of those electronic fences — step out of line and they'll zap you."

"How long have you worked for Decode?" Grace asked, wanting to change the subject. She didn't like the trapped feeling his words were imparting.

"I was a Drakian at first. Gene Drake, the guy who first tried to blow the whistle on the bar code tattoo, was my housemate for a while. But I switched to Decode. They're not as dramatic, but I think they're more effective."

Grace pointed to the book of maps spread out in front of him. "What are you doing there?"

"Ever hear of The Bar Code Prophecy?"

From the way he asked, Grace knew he had no idea about her connection to the prophecy. And she wasn't about to tell him.

"I've heard of it, yes," she said.

"Well, Decode is studying the native American Indian lands. We're looking especially at the sacred Hopi places. We think if we can find the second tablet of The Bar Code Prophecy, it might help us fight Global-1." Nate shifted his position and pushed his hair back pensively. "Personally, I think it's got to be underground somewhere. The Hopi had ceremonial dwellings built into the earth. Kivas."

Grace remembered Eric's terrifying climb down Spider Rock to the opening holding the first half of the prophecy. "That makes sense," she agreed.

Harry Clemente came out of a room and approached her. "The boss wants to talk to you," he told Grace.

Nate's eyes widened. "Big day, Grace. You're about to meet David Young."

"The head of Decode?"

"Yep."

Grace followed Harry Clemente into a spare, unadorned office. Behind a metal desk sat a thinly muscular man in his forties, wearing jeans and a plaid shirt. A bristly gray and white beard covered the lower half of his chiseled face. Dark eyes sparkled at her. "Welcome, Grace," David Young said, standing and extending a hand to shake. "It's so good to meet you. I'm pleased that you've become a Postman."

Just six months earlier, Grace recalled, Global-1 had nearly killed David Young with their nanobot technology. She had read all about how they'd jailed him and used the tiny robots to stimulate his vagus nerve until it induced thoughts of suicide. Now, though, he struck her as vigorous and bristling with energy, warm and open and intense.

David Young came around and leaned against his desk, inviting Grace to sit on a nearby desk chair. He handed her back the manila envelope Jack had given her. "You've met Jack Kelly?" he inquired.

"Yes," Grace confirmed. "And his partner, Allyson."

"Geniuses, the both of them. My father and I are thrilled to fund them. Not only do we agree that magnetic repulsion technology will be the way to provide free energy for all people, we don't want Global-1 to wind up getting a part of their work. It's too important to humanity."

"Jack and Allyson would never sell out to Global-1," Grace replied. She hadn't known them long, but she felt certain this was true.

"Global-1 is tricky," David Young countered. "They have lots of small subsidiary companies posing as independents, but they all belong to Global-1. They own whole countries."

"What countries?" Grace asked, shocked.

"They're small countries . . . so far. They're thinking bigger these days."

"America?" Grace guessed.

"They're almost there," David Young said with a nod. "They own lots of our lawmakers already. That's why my father can't get anywhere with his investigation."

"Is it hopeless?"

David Young's face grew serious. "I don't know. Maybe. We're starting to think so. It's why The Bar Code Prophecy might be our last hope. That's why I wanted to meet you. Eutonah feels somehow that you are the key. She told me about taking you and her son, Eric, to Spider Rock."

"Do you believe in prophecies?" Grace asked him. She still wasn't sure that she did.

"Not normally," David Young admitted. "I'm not superstitious. But I've studied this, and so many of the Hopi prophecies have come to pass. I remember when British Petroleum dumped all that oil in the Gulf, killing so much wildlife. The Hopi predicted that. We're watching it — carefully. That's all I can say. And that's why we've been watching you."

"Is there something I'm supposed to do?" Grace asked.

"Could be," David Young said. There was something in the way he said it that made Grace nervous. It was as though he was taking her measure, deciding if she was ready to hear what he had to say next.

"I've loaded the fake bar code in that envelope with a great deal of money. I want Jack Kelly and Allyson Minor to set up shop in the Great Basin Desert where he started out, at the Decode caves there. He can run the whole operation on solar power. He knows how and there's no shortage of sun. I want you and Eric to go stay with him in the caves."

"Why?" Grace asked.

"Eutonah tells me there will be a gathering of the tribes at Big Mountain. The tribal elders believe that the time has come for The Bar Code Prophecy to be fulfilled. They believe that somehow the presence of the Brother and his love, the Daughter of the Master of Destruction, will deliver the people."

"His love," Grace echoed softly.

David Young heard her and smiled gently. "I don't know what will happen, Grace. What I'm asking might take a lot of courage. I can't be sure. But in my gut, I feel that's where you should be. It's where we all need you to be."

"Do you know what's happened to my family — the one I was raised with?" Grace asked. "I don't want to go before I find out."

"The Postman didn't tell you?" David Young seemed surprised.

"He wanted to, but the Global-1 police came between us. Is he all right? Eric Chaca is out looking for him now."

"If you don't hear from Eric soon, get word to us. We have a Postman out there who knows where they are, but we usually let the Postmen run themselves. It's safer that way. If there's no central headquarters, Global-1 can't raid it. I give you my personal promise that I will keep tabs on this and get word to you."

David Young seemed like a man she could trust. He had insisted on staying in jail until every last resister picked up in the D.C. raid of the last year had been freed.

"All right," Grace agreed. "If you keep looking for my family, I'll go."

David Young extended his hand to shake and Grace took it. "I give you my word," he said.

When Grace was once more out on the street, the manila envelope tucked in the back waistband of her jeans and under her T-shirt, she headed back toward the subway station, completely lost in thought. What was going to happen? She'd been only four years old during the Mayan calendar doomsday scare of 2012. Nothing had happened, and people laughed about it now. But was Eutonah right? Was the creation of the bar code tattoo the thing that had actually happened in 2012? Had it set in motion a series of events that were now unfolding?

Shielding her eyes, Grace tried to look at the sky but had to turn away. The bright yellow was overlaid with a haze of dirty smog. She saw the sign for the subway just two blocks away on the other side and she cut a diagonal across the street, heading for it. At least her first mission had gone well. Jack and Allyson would be pleased to have so much money for their swing-lo project. Maybe Eric would be there when she returned to the garage and would have news about her family.

As Grace crossed, she noticed two uniformed Global-1 police officers were walking down the street toward her. When she reached the other side she would walk right past them.

Her heartbeat quickened and, to be safe, she turned back to the side of the street she'd just left. There was something in their purposeful stride that had alarmed her.

Without waiting to reach the corner, the officers crossed, fanning out.

Now on high alert, Grace turned back toward Decode headquarters. The G-1 cops began walking with aggressive strides in the same direction.

A drone helicopter appeared in the lemon sky between two skyscrapers.

How had they found her? Grace's growing fear caused her heart to hammer in her chest. The pounding reminded her of her circulation. The nanochip had most likely circulated outside the jacket's protection. In moments the signal would be blocked by the jacket once more.

The signal jammer was in her pocket, and Grace used it now.

But they'd already established visual contact. It was too late.

Shot threw with adrenaline-fueled fear, Grace broke into an all-out run and the G-1 police did the same. They would soon outrun her. This was the time to use all the free-running skills Eric had taught her.

Remembering Eric's advice, she shut down conscious thought and let her body take over. Leaping, she landed catlike on a railing and then sprang to a low window ledge, gripping with her fingers.

"Grace Morrow! Freeze!" The words boomed from one of the officers on the street below. "Global-1 Police."

Without a backward glance Grace found her footing on a window ledge and moved swiftly to the right until she came to a window that was slightly open. With her foot she lifted it and slipped inside, racing through the apartment, jumping over children sprawled on the floor watching TV.

Out in the hall, she ran toward the stairs, only to see four G-1 cops running up. Reversing directions, she sprinted up a staircase to the roof.

The G-1 drone helicopter hovered there in anticipation of her arrival. A red dot played on her chest as the drone sought its target. Grace launched into a forward flip to elude the robotic predator as red laser light scorched the side of her shoulder. The flip brought her to the edge of the building. There was a lower roof, but a leap was required.

The four G-1 police raced out the roof doorway.

Backing up several paces, Grace sprang forward, kicking her arms and legs to drive her body forward, and landed on her side, rolling to standing. She was by the door of this rooftop and ran for it, but found it locked. Looking over the side, she found a fire escape that she was able to drop to and scramble down. She made it to the alley and saw no sign of her pursuers.

But they would soon be upon her. They probably knew where she was already. Grace spied a basement window and, seizing a broken brick in the alley, smashed it so she could reach in and unlock it. Maneuvering carefully through the broken glass, she scraped her arm anyway as she slipped into the basement, landing on top of a closed washing machine. Her coat was torn and the blood ran in a stream down her arm. Wiping the blood, she thought of the nanobots in it sending signals into space even as they escaped her body.

The blades of the drone helicopter flapped overhead.

Grace checked that the envelope from David Young was still tucked into the waistband of her jeans and was relieved to find it there.

On the far wall of the large basement were two doors and Grace headed for them. One led to a staircase going up. The other led into a cool, windowless room containing the building's plumbing and piled with dirt. There was no sense going up again. They'd only grab her.

Locking the basement door leading to the staircase, Grace crawled into the dirt room. Pulling her knees to her chest, she sat and waited until the sound of the whirring chopper blades receded, all the while knowing that as soon as she went out again, they might return.

Grace's stomach rumbled with hunger as she pushed open the door of the dirt room and re-entered the dark basement. She couldn't stay there all night. She'd simply have to try to find her way back to the garage. Hopefully the blackness of night would help and the jammer would work. She had to pray that the nanochip in her blood wouldn't begin broadcasting a signal the moment she emerged from underground.

The building she was in seemed quiet as she stole up the dimly let staircase to the first floor. A man came into the lobby, holding his jacket over his shoulder, sweating from the heat he'd just left behind in the street. "Wow, it's hot out!" he said to her as he punched a number into his cell phone.

"Sure is," Grace replied casually.

He eyed the cut on her arm. "That looks like it hurts," he remarked. "Better clean it up."

"I will," Grace agreed, heading for the front door.

The man suddenly cursed and banged his cell phone with his other hand. Grace whirled toward him to see what the problem could be. "I haven't been able to get a call through all day," he explained angrily. "These solar flares are jamming everything."

Not everything, Grace thought as she pushed the door open and left the building. Apparently Global-1 had stronger equipment than the average person.

Outside the sky glowed eerily, almost as though the sun were still making its way through the blackness of night. The heat was no better than it had been during the day. Checking that she still had the manila envelope, Grace made her way down the front steps onto the street, her eyes darting in every direction, alert for any sign she was being trailed.

"Grace," a female voice hissed.

Startled, Grace turned. Kayla's back was to the side wall of an alley. Reaching out, she snapped Grace into the alley beside her. "Thank God, I found you. We all came out looking for you as soon as we saw the commotion. Did they come for you?"

Grace nodded. "It was close," she reported.

"I'll bet." In a quick jog, Kayla headed down the alley. "Come on. We're all leaving."

Grace followed close behind. "Where are we going?"

"To the desert. Hurry. We were just waiting on you. We're already way behind schedule."

Pasadena Sun
August 8, 2026 — Bedford Hills, New York

CHEROKEE BAR CODE DISSIDENT RELEASED FROM JAIL. CALLS FOR SUMMIT OF NATIVE AMERICAN SHAMANS AND CHIEFTAINS

In her first press conference upon being released from the all-women Bedford Hills Correctional Facility in Bedford

Hills, New York, the Cherokee Medicine Woman and shaman known only as Eutonah thanked former Senator Ambrose Young, who had worked vigilantly for her freedom. "He has become a great friend to our cause," she told the press and followers who had assembled to hear her.

Her second statement called for Native American leaders to send delegations to a summit to be held on Hopi and Navajo lands near Sedona, Arizona. "This too-bright sun means the time is upon us," she said enigmatically. When questioned on the meaning of her words, Eutonah said only, "The people have long awaited the time that all the prophecies have foretold since the beginning of this world. We must be ready to engage our hearts, minds, and spirits to face the inevitable changes." When pressed to say what these "changes" might be, Eutonah refused to elaborate, but added, "Companies have been strip-mining this land for almost a hundred years. First it was coal and minerals, then oil. Most recently it's the uranium. And last year they found lithium deposits out there."

When it was pointed out that native peoples have allowed this by selling mining rights, she answered, "Back in the last century the Navajo were so impoverished that they sold some of the mining rights. That's true, but the company they sold the rights to mined to an extent that was never imagined by the native Indians. Back in 2014, Global-1 bought up every small mining company with a contract out there; now they're spreading into Hopi territory. In the last five years, Global-1 has also spread into Utah, onto the lands of the Ute, Shoshone, and Paiute nations. It's completely destroying the land."

When asked to speak to the feelings of the tribal nations on this issue, Eutonah told the assembled crowd, "The native people are protesting like crazy. A Tribal Council has gone to D.C., believing that the entire balance of the universe has been upset because all these minerals are being pulled out of the ground. The members of the council say that by taking the minerals out of the earth there, the very bio-electric balance of the universe has been thrown off-kilter. They are not speaking in the mystical abstract here. They are talking about science: radioactivity, magnetism, and the tidal and gravitational balance that the heavenly bodies maintain in relation to each other."

When asked to comment, President Loudon Waters claimed that the Cherokee leader was merely trying to frighten people in order to keep her movement vital. "Every problem with the bar code tattoo has been ironed out. This woman no longer has a reason to exist. She's simply looking to extend her fame and influence in a world where her movement has become irrelevant."

In response, Eutonah stated, "Loudon Waters does not speak for the people, not my people or those of any other race or nationality. He speaks only for the greed of his own group. The people of this planet need to know that the last days of prophecy are upon us. The time is now."

PART FOUR

"We are part of everything that is beneath us, above us, around us."

— Winona LaDuke, Ojibwe, 1999

"Water Spirit feelin' springin' 'round my head
Makes me glad that I'm not dead."

"Witchi Tai To," written by Jim Pepper of Kaw and Creek Native American descent from a song handed down to him by his grandfather and father.

SEVENTEEN

Grace stepped out to the mouth of the cave, careful to stay back in its shade. The Decode station gave shelter not only from the blasting sun but also blocked the signal the nanochip in her blood were bouncing onto satellites in the sky — if they were indeed getting through the powerful solar flares. She surveyed the expanse of desert in front of her. It seemed to her that off in the distance she could see something that shimmered and reflected the sun. Turning, she saw Kayla come alongside her.

"Is there water out there?" Grace asked, pointing.

"It's a mirage," Kayla replied, shielding her eyes as she studied the horizon. "It's an optical illusion, a trick of the heat and the light. But I always like to think it's the ghost of the sea."

"What do you mean?"

Kayla turned to Grace and smiled softly. "Millions of years ago there was a seaway that came through here, splitting the continent. As the waters receded, they left these deserts. There are fossils of shells all over the place out here. I've seen them myself."

That the Earth was so very old was something Grace found almost impossible to imagine. She tried to think of an ocean in the spot she was looking at. Without too much effort she could imagine it. The vastness of the desert seemed made to accommodate an ocean.

"It does look like an ocean out there. I see it, too," Kayla said.

Grace turned to her sharply, surprised.

Kayla laughed, amused by Grace's shocked expression. "I can see what you're thinking because I'm a telepath," Kayla explained. "You knew that, didn't you?"

Grace remembered seeing Kayla and Mfumbe communicating mind to mind back in the garage. "Can you see into anyone's mind?" Grace asked.

"Most of the time," Kayla replied. "Just like you, I imagine the ocean out here. It's a vision I have all the time."

"But aren't your visions of the future?" Grace inquired. "That would be a vision of the past."

"I know. I don't understand it."

Eric came out from the cave and stood between Kayla and Grace. He had arrived the night before, after Grace was already asleep. He put his hand on her shoulder.

"We've found your family," he said.

Closing her eyes, Grace sighed with relief and happiness. The pleased look on Eric's face told her they were all right, that this wasn't bad news.

"Where are they?" she asked him.

"Decode headquarters in the Adirondacks."

"But why . . . how . . . what are they doing there?" Grace stammered, confused.

Dr. Harriman emerged from the cave. "I can answer that."

"Dr. Harriman!" Grace cried. "What happened to you?"

"After fighting my way down out of the tree tops, do you mean?" he asked. "After that ordeal, I contacted your father — I mean the father who raised you, of course."

"You know my father, then."

"Growing up, he was my best friend. Who else would I trust with my only child? I never doubted he would love you as his own."

"How did you contact him?"

"It was I who tipped your family to flee to the Adirondacks. I knew Global-1 was coming to pick them up. I thought you would make it home sooner and that Global-1 wouldn't arrive until later — that there would be time for all of you to escape together. But I was wrong. So I told them I would have Decode come pick up Grace and that they should go ahead."

"You work with Decode?" Eric asked, aghast at the news.

"Once I saw how Global-1 was using my work, I wanted no part of it. When I saw how they were treating Kathryn Reed, Grace's biological mother, I was doubly horrified."

"Wait a minute," Kayla interrupted. "My grandmother was named Kathryn Reed. She's my adoptive father's mother, but she's actually my biological mother because her eggs were used to conceive me and the other five clones."

"That's right," Dr. Harriman said. "I loved Kathryn and you, Grace, are our child. But when I learned that they wanted to use your embryo for experiments — as they did on Kayla — we were determined not to let it happen."

"How did you stop them?" Kayla asked.

"Your mother — the one who adopted you, Grace — was pregnant but had just suffered a miscarriage. I persuaded an obstetrician friend of mine to secretly remove the embryo from Kathryn and implant it in your mother. Your mother carried you to term in her belly while we told Global-1 that Kathryn had miscarried."

"Then why have they been watching me?" Grace asked.

"They never really believed it," Dr. Harriman admitted. "That's why they were hovering, waiting for you to be tattooed so they could match our DNA conclusively."

"Wait! Wait!" Kayla cried, holding up her hands to slow the flow of his narrative. "Are you saying that Grace and I are sisters?"

"Half sisters," Dr. Harriman said. "Same mother, different father."

Grace and Kayla studied each other. There *were* some similarities that Grace could see. She certainly looked more like Kayla than she did Kim.

"What is their problem with you, Dr. Harriman?" Eric asked. "They think you're one of them, don't they?"

"They're onto me. They have been ever since we claimed Grace was never born. But they couldn't do anything because I still knew things no one else knew. And I was helping them, in ways that I had to. Now they want my latest experiment, but I refuse to give it to them, or even admit it exists for that matter."

"What is it?" Kayla asked.

"It's a secret," Dr. Harriman replied, turning back into the cave. "It's better that you don't know."

Katie's tractor trailer pulled past the front of the cave. Grace followed Eric, Kayla, and several other members of Decode who were staying in the cave as they ran out to meet it. The back truck doors opened and Jack handed five-gallon jugs of water to the waiting hands of those below.

Mfumbe and Katie descended from the cab and walked toward the back. "Mission accomplished," Mfumbe announced as he embraced Kayla happily. "Water and a fresh load of fake tattoos from the town of Baker."

Allyson stood beside Jack inside the truck, which was stacked full of boxes. "And all the equipment we need to start producing the first ever magnetic repulsion-fueled flying machines," she announced, gesturing triumphantly toward the boxes.

"Swing low, sweet chariot, comin' for to carry me home!" Jack sang out the old gospel tune for which he'd named his invention. As he sang, he began handing down the boxes.

"Where do you want us to put these, Jack?" Eric asked.

"Just inside the cave," Jack replied. "I'm going to use the swing-lo to fly the materials up to one of these tabletop mesas and set up shop there. We can fly from mesa top to mesa top without having to land on the ground below. I want to see if I can fly higher if I start higher."

"Better pack a chute," Eric warned, grinning at Grace.

"Every swing-lo will come equipped with two parachutes," Allyson said as she handed Grace a box. "You can count on that."

Grace joined Eric as they carried their boxes into the cave. "Have you heard from your mother since she got out of jail?" she asked him.

Eric nodded as he set his box down. "I was just going to talk to you about that," he said. "She wants us to meet her in the old Hopi village of Walpi, on the first mesa of the Hopi reservation. We can take one of the motorcycles there."

"When does she want us there?"

"Tomorrow at sunrise."

"Do you know why?"

"It has to do with the prophecy," Eric told her. Grace walked closer to the opening of the cave. The sun beat on her and the thought of putting on that foil-lined jacket was unbearable. "I can't go, Eric. I can't wear that jacket in this heat, and without it, they'll come for me."

"Perhaps I can help," said Dr. Harriman, coming to join them from the back of the cave. He held a device resembling a remote control. "It's Global-1's most powerful signal jammer. Nothing less will totally block the signal that is coming from your bloodstream."

"I can use it?" Grace asked hopefully.

Dr. Harriman handed it to her. "Yes, but be warned that you will block every signal in your area. If you need medical emergency assistance, no one will be able to call for it. Police won't be able to communicate. You will even knock out phones in the area. So turn it off whenever you're somewhere safe."

"Is this the technology you've been working on?" Eric asked.

"I've deconstructed how this works," Dr. Harriman said, "but Global-1's satellite division built it. What I'm working on is much more complex than a signal jammer."

"Can't you tell us?" Grace urged him.

"It's not a hundred percent perfected," Dr. Harriman revealed.

"Why does Global-1 want it so badly?" Eric questioned.

"It will break their hold on the people of the Earth," Dr. Harriman said, his blue eyes darkening with emotion. "It will change everything."

Despite the heat, icy fear ran up Grace's spine. The time of The Bar Code Prophecy seemed to be getting closer. What would it mean for her, for all of them?

Looking out of the cave, Grace saw that the blazing yellow sky seemed even brighter than it had the day before. What was this strange light? What did it mean?

To get to Hopi territory, Eric and Grace had to first drive through Navajo lands. As they approached Monument Valley on Highway 163, Grace was overwhelmed by the breathtaking landscape. The red-brown earth tones of immense rectangular buttes and other towering rock formations sat against the soaring blue expanse of sky. It was the most awe-inspiring location she'd ever seen. And now that she knew her family was safe, she allowed herself to actually enjoy it.

Eric leaned back and shouted to be heard from beneath his helmet and over the roar of the motorcycle engine. "Amazing, huh?"

"Amazing," she echoed, thinking that the word didn't seem to half capture the majestic forms and deep colors surrounding her. For the first time ever, Grace understood what might be meant by the term *sacred lands*. These rocks and lands emanated a solemnity that was beyond description.

Several hours later, Eric pulled off the highway. "You must need some water and lunch by now," he guessed, taking off his helmet and ruffling his hair.

"Look at this," Grace said, turning in a slow circle to take it all in. "I never imagined anything could be this overpowering. I feel like I'm on a different planet."

"I know."

They sat cross-legged eating the bread and fruit they'd packed, sipping from their water bottles. Grace tugged on the brim of the cap she'd brought, glad to have it to protect her face from the blistering sun. The heat waves lifting up from the ground reminded Grace of her conversation with Kayla, about how a seaway had once flowed over this desert. She understood Kayla's idea that its remains could be found in this liquid desert mirage.

As she gazed into the waves of heat coming off the highway, Grace realized that the ground beneath her was shaking. An earthquake?

Eric stood, letting his lunch tumble from his lap. Grace got up beside him and he wrapped his arm around her protectively. Grace looked to him. "What is it?"

Responding with a puzzled shake of his head, Eric snapped up the motorcycle helmets they'd left on the ground. They headed for the bike, but before they reached it, they were hit with a thundering wind. Dust and rocks spattered them. Something huge but invisible was thundering by. "What was *that*?!" Grace cried, once whatever had passed was far enough away to make hearing possible.

Eric brushed gravel and red dirt from her back and sleeves. "Is your signal jammer on?"

Grace's hand flew to her mouth. "I don't know. I shut it off when we had breakfast in the underground parking garage

under that mall. I can't remember if I turned it back on."
Fishing it from her backpack she discovered it was off. "How
did you know it wasn't on?"

"I was just guessing. But *something* gigantic just passed us.
And if it was using stealth-cloaking technology, the jammer
should have disrupted it. That's why I asked if it was off."

Grace clicked the jammer back on. "All this time they could
have been tracking me," she said. "I wonder why they haven't."

Pasadena Sun
August 12, 2026

Solar Flares Disrupt Communications Between Space Stations

NASA has reported that its formerly manned space station has been completely evacuated of both its U.S. and
Russian staff. The last personnel from the space stations
run by China and Pakistan boarded space shuttles today.
Global-1 Station is the only one that has not yet been
evacuated.

"These precautions have been undertaken as Meteor
1 quickly approaches Earth," Gus Hardy, a NASA representative, stated at a press conference yesterday.
"Although its trajectory is still calculated to bypass
Earth, the space stations themselves are considered to be
at risk. This risk has been amplified by the fact that

unusual solar activity has disrupted communication signals both here on Earth and in space. "Drone technology is especially in jeopardy since it depends on transmitted signal devices," Hardy went on to say. "Disruption of these signals on the scale that we are currently experiencing could prove disastrous."

The Federal Communications Commission (FCC) warns that citizens might also be experiencing difficulty with smart phones, e-mail, and other electronic devices disrupted by solar flares. "Be prepared for static on the line and dropped calls to a greater degree than normal," Beth McGhee, an FCC spokesperson, stated. "We have even seen disruption in the use of electronic passes at toll booths."

Neither spokesperson was willing to comment on how long this disruptive activity is likely to last.

EIGHTEEN

Eric drove his motorcycle up the sloped road leading into the abandoned city of Walpi, atop the first mesa in Hopi territory. Seated behind him, Grace squinted into the glare of first morning sun bouncing off the flat rooflines of the square, ancient adobe homes stacked one upon the other in three tiers.

Eutonah was already there, standing on the flat stone that created a sort of courtyard in front of the tiered homes. With her was a Native American in a traditional feather headdress. His skin was tanned and deeply lined but his posture was youthfully erect.

Stopping the motorcycle in front of them, Eric locked it into its stand and went to embrace the man and then his mother. "Grace, this is my uncle Russell, who raised me," Eric introduced the man. "Uncle Russ, this is my very good friend, Grace Morrow."

Grace extended her hand and Uncle Russell clasped it in his two strong, rough palms. "The Daughter," he said, turning her wrist so that her bar code tattoo was revealed. "The lines your father has carved in your arm will pull down the sky." His voice was level, thoughtful. Grace didn't perceive any judgment or blame in it, only a statement of fact.

His words chilled her. *Pull down the sky?* What did that mean?

"Where are the others?" Eric asked Eutonah.

"They are gathering at Canyon de Chelly. We will join them later, but I have had a vision. Chief Russ is the only one I've told of it, and he has dreamed similar things."

"The knowingness has come in a dream," Chief Russell stated, "just as it was foretold."

"What have you seen?" Eric asked.

"Here is where we will find the second part of the prophecy," Eutonah told them. She beckoned for them to follow her back toward the stacked cubed village. The too-bright sun made the mottled adobe walls glow with an iridescent yellow. Beads of sweat were already forming on Grace's forehead and upper lip.

They followed Eutonah into the shade of an adobe building on the first level. The shadowy, empty space was low but expansive, seeming larger than an ordinary home. Eutonah led them down a narrow ladder into a lower tier. She didn't speak until they had all come down the ladder. "This is a kiva," she explained, "a sacred underground place of worship. It is well-known that this is here." Again, she beckoned for them to follow her, leading them to a stone bench at the far end of the kiva. Kneeling, she threw all her weight into pushing the bench. Eric and Grace dropped down beside her, lending their help.

Grace was sweating with the effort before she felt the stone budge. Encouraged by the movement, the three of them exerted all their strength, forcing the stone bench to move nearly three feet. Eutonah rocked back on her heels and gave a cry of elation. "It is exactly what I saw in my vision!"

Getting onto her belly, Grace peered into the darkness of the opening below the stone bench. Eric joined her, flashing a pen light into the vast, black hole. "The mesa is hollow," Eric concluded.

Grace looked up to Eutonah. "Are you saying the rest of The Bar Code Prophecy is down there?"

Eutonah pointed toward a pile of climbing ropes and equipment in the kiva. "I brought these down earlier. There are a rope and a halter for each of you," she said.

Grace stared at Eutonah, speechless.

"You're kidding, right?" Eric said.

"I've never been more serious," Eutonah replied. "Your uncle agrees with me. The rest of the prophecy is down there."

"You are the Brother. I know because in my dream vision it was you who held the missing piece of the tablet," Chief Russell added.

"In your vision was I alive or dead?" Eric asked, his joking manner only barely disguising his fear.

"I could not tell," Chief Russell admitted in a matter-of-fact tone.

"And if I don't find anything, does it mean I'm not the Brother?" Eric asked, getting to his feet.

"Yes," Chief Russell replied.

"Okay then," Eric said, heading for the pile of climbing gear. "Let's get this over with. Frankly, it's so dark down there that I don't think I'll find a thing. And I wouldn't mind not being the Brother. It's more responsibility than I'm really in the mood for right now."

"This is nothing to joke about, son," Eutonah scolded.

"Who's joking?" Eric asked as he pulled on a climbing halter.

As they went back and forth, Grace silently got into her own halter. Eric had spent enough time watching her back — now it was time for her to return the favor.

"Whoa, Grace," Eric said when he finally saw her. "You're not coming. It is way too dangerous."

"There are two halters here," Grace argued, looking to Eutonah for support. "You meant me to go down there, too, didn't you, Eutonah?"

"It is foretold that the Daughter and the Brother must work in accord," Eutonah said.

"Mom!" Eric protested. "We have no idea what's down there. The walls could be crumbling. We don't even know how deep it is or where this tablet could be."

"You need Grace," Eutonah insisted.

"I can do it," Grace said to Eric. "You yourself told me I was one of the best climbers you'd ever met."

Eric gave in. "All right. Let's do it."

Grace looked to Eutonah for confirmation and Eutonah gave it with a nod. Clicking off her signal jammer — there would be no need for it as she descended deep into this rock — Grace was swept with the feeling that what she was about to do was somehow the most important thing she had ever attempted in her life.

NINETEEN

Grace hung in midair from a climbing rope tied to a pillar in the kiva. Around her was complete blackness.

"Grace!"

"Where are you, Eric?"

A flood light snapped on from the opening above, making Grace blink and turn from the sudden light. Eric hung just feet away. Instinctively they reached for each other, their fingers intertwining.

"Are you all right?" Eutonah shouted as she moved the light's beam around, revealing rock walls in the immense opening. It was comforting to be able to see something in this world of infinite quiet and total darkness. They had come with flashlights clipped to their harnesses, but Eutonah's light was brighter and cast a broader beam.

Grace inhaled deeply to calm her nerves. The air was cool and helped her to focus. There was a narrow ledge running along the surface of the closest section of the rock wall. With a tap to his shoulder, she pointed it out to Eric.

"Over there!" Eutonah shouted down. "There's an opening in the rock. I saw something like it in my vision. Try to get to it."

Still holding hands, Eric and Grace rocked their bodies

back and forth until they were swinging wide. Soon they were bouncing onto the edge of the ridge but unable to grab hold. Separating, they swung — kicking off and swinging back — slowing at each interval until the movement was a controlled bounce. Finally, Grace spied some jutting rock and reached for it with two hands, gripping until she could pull her entire weight onto the ledge. Eric did the same, landing about three feet farther away. With her face turned to the side, Grace inched toward the opening in the wall. Eric quickly caught up to her and was right behind.

As Grace was about to enter, she felt a tug at her waist and was unable to go farther. "You don't have any more line," Eric told her. "Me neither. We have to unhook."

Grace peered at the carabiner tethering her to her climbing line and then to Eric. This line was all that connected her to the world above.

"It's okay," Eric assured her, holding her line. "We'll keep the lines."

Reluctant but knowing there was no choice, Grace unclipped. Eric still held her line as he unhooked his own. Clipping the two lines together, he looped them around an out-cropping of rock.

"They'll be there when we come out," he promised. Then, looking up, he shouted to Eutonah, "Mom! Keep as much light on this opening as you can."

Grace led the way as they made their way into the opening. Grace could stand with only inches of room above her head. Eric needed to stoop. He took out his light and swept it around the cavelike opening.

Grace gasped at what his light revealed. Sleeping bats clung to the walls. The light made several of them stir, forcing Grace to fight down panic. What if they all awoke at once and began swarming the cave?

Eric shone the beam on the floor and put his finger to his lip. With his light still down, he moved stealthily around the cave, searching for any kind of stone tablet. Grace moved beside him, scanning the rock floor, trying to block out the occasional chitter of a bat they had half roused.

There was nothing there. They would have to continue searching elsewhere. Grace did not relish the prospect of going any farther into this frightening black space.

"Let's get out of here," she whispered.

"Okay," he agreed. "I just want to look at this mark here on the wall." Cupping the light from his flashlight to avoid disturbing the sleeping bats, Eric held it to the back of the cave wall. "It's a circle," he observed, stepping closer to it. "So people did come —"

Eric suddenly tottered backward as the ground under his feet gave way.

Grace grabbed his arm to keep him from falling over, but his weight only pulled her forward.

In the next second, they were both falling through darkness.

"Grace, are you all right?"

Lifting her arms, Grace probed the complete darkness for Eric and found his face. "My knee really hurts," she replied, wincing. "What about you?"

He flicked on his flashlight, revealing a lower section of the cave. The floor they had fallen through was about fifteen feet above them. Above them the bats were swirling frantically, distressed by the sound of the crash, squeaking and flapping their wings.

"I'm okay," he said. "I hit my head but it's not bleeding."

Eric swung his light beam around the space. Clay plates, jugs, and urns — some broken, others intact — were strewn across the earthen floor. Grace saw where her flashlight had rolled and crawled to it. Adding her light to Eric's, she saw a pictograph on the wall.

"Eric, look," she said.

"It's like some kind of timeline," Eric observed as they stood studying it. A large stick figure of a man stood to the left. At his feet was a horizontal line with various markings on it — small drawings that seemed to indicate various events. The last one showed a boat with squiggly black marks pouring downward. "This could be the British Petroleum oil spill back in 2010," Eric said.

"It keeps going, though," Grace observed, sweeping her light to the right. There was a thick black vertical line crossing the horizontal timeline and jagged lines emanating from the center crossing marks. One line reached all the way to a circle ringed with a corona of fire.

"I wonder if that represents Big Mountain at the sacred Four Corners," Eric said, shining his light on it. He turned to Grace. "The Four Corners is where Arizona, New Mexico, Utah, and Colorado meet. My people consider it a spot of very high energy, the most sacred place."

"But that's where they're mining," Grace said, recalling the line of Global-1 mining trucks.

"Let's keep looking for the other piece of the tablet," Eric suggested, moving his light from the wall and surveying the rest of the space with its light.

Grace crouched low to the ground and tried to get a closer look at the dishware there. It was white and had various figures of strange creatures etched into it. Eric joined her, inspecting the engravings on the clay. "I wish we knew what this all means," he said, picking up the broken half of a dish.

Grace shined her flashlight in his direction to illuminate him as he spoke and she noticed the piece he held. "Look at the inscription on that pottery you're holding," she said, shining her light directly on it. "It's a small version of the picture on the wall but it goes on even longer."

Eric checked the pictograph in his hand. "You're right."

They looked at each other excitedly. "I don't think this is a plate, either," Eric added, turning it. "It's completely flat."

"And broken at the top," Grace added. "Do you think it could be the other half of the prophecy?"

Eric stood, still inspecting the broken pottery. "What I think is that we should get this back to my uncle right away."

"How are we going to get out of here?" Grace asked. The cave wall curved up to the ceiling, and the opening they had made when they crashed through was at the center. "Even you can't climb upside down."

"Get on my shoulders," Eric suggested, crouching. But when Eric was standing, clutching Grace's ankles, she still could only touch the top with the tips of her fingers. Her attempt to jump up sent them both crashing to the ground as the ancient ceiling crumbled under her grasp.

A bat flew down and swirled around the room, making Grace cover her head. And then suddenly it was gone. "It didn't fly back up," Grace said to Eric. "I was watching the opening."

Three more bats descended and disappeared the same way. The next time it happened, Eric trained his light on them, following their exit path. "Come on," he said. "They sense some way out."

At the far end of the space, they found an opening just large enough to fit into. Grace swallowed hard as nerves threatened her. Where did it lead? Would they get stuck? But then she realized: They didn't really have any other option. With a new-found determination, she pushed herself into the opening. Eric followed.

They crawled through complete darkness. Occasionally a bat whizzed past them, making Grace flatten to let it go by. In about fifteen minutes, Grace heard a sound ahead of them, but couldn't tell what it was. It might be rushing water, but it seemed louder than that. It encouraged her that they were coming close to something at the other end. "I think we're almost there," Eric called ahead to her.

The tunnel let out in a large cavern with stalactites and stalagmites that met in the middle to form columns. More bats roosted in the ceiling and side walls, while some flew in from other openings. Eric and Grace followed the sounds in a downward slope until they were sloshing through knee-deep water that gradually grew more and more shallow.

Grace squinted into a shard of light. Reaching out, Eric took her hand as they walked toward the opening of the cave, the sunlight growing ever more blinding. Slowly their eyes adjusted.

There was nothing there.

And yet something was making the sounds of motors and engines. There was a tremendous gust of wind.

All at once, as if out of nowhere, the cloak of invisibility was lifted.

Stretching for as far as Grace could see, Global-1 trucks and machinery gouged the land, clanking as they dug. Blackened water ran down high sluices continuing along miles of above-ground pipe. High in the air, Global-1 drone helicopters hovered, their whirling blades glinting in the sunlight. Uniformed Global-1 police brandished laser rifles as they patrolled the perimeter.

Still holding hands, Grace and Eric backed up, not wanting to be detected. Abruptly, they collided with Eutonah and Chief Russell, who had come up behind them.

"How did you get here?" Eric asked.

"Uncle Russ knows a path around the mesa. We drove until the road ended and then we hiked," Eutonah told him. "When we saw you weren't coming up, we figured you'd try to come all the way down, and we wanted to meet you. I can't believe what we've uncovered here."

"You've jammed their stealth cloaking signals!" Eric realized.

Eutonah held out the signal jammer. "This thing is powerful," she said. "I heard the noises and thought I'd give it a try."

"Unbelievable," Grace murmured, taking in the massive mining operation.

The Global-1 workers were descending from their machines and trucks, realizing that they were visible. Voices rose in alarm as they tried to contact each other and discovered that their phones wouldn't work.

Eutonah pointed the jammer at the scene once more. A strange glistening descended on everything and then it snapped out of sight as quickly as it had appeared. "I don't want to tip them off that we've seen them," she explained. "At least not yet. Hopefully, they'll think it was just some sort of solar flare glitch."

Chief Russell seemed unaware that the machines and trucks and equipment had disappeared. He stared at the place where they had been, his formerly serene face now twisted into an expression of horror.

"They are destroying the universe," he said.

"It fits," Chief Russell said as they sat deep in the interior of the cave in a shadowy section under the mesa. "This is the part of the prophecy we now call The Bar Code Prophecy." He placed the piece Eric had picked up and locked it into place with the earlier tablet that had been retrieved from the side of Spider Rock.

"What does it say?" Eutonah asked.

He drew his fingers along the horizontal line. "This is now and here's where the line divides. This is the path of respecting the Earth, our mother. It is the path that humans have not taken. This jagged line ascending to the sun will be our destiny now."

Eric pointed to a stick figure of a man climbing the jagged line. "What does this mean, Uncle?"

"I do not pretend to know what will happen. But there is a meteor currently in our orbit," Chief Russell replied.

"But it's supposed to miss us," Grace said anxiously. "All the scientists say it will pass us by."

"This man is climbing high," Chief Russell said, tapping the figure on the pictograph. "It's probably good advice for all of us."

"We have to tell what we know," Eric said urgently. "The world has to be made aware of this. It will affect everyone."

Eutonah nodded pensively. "Global-1 controls all the TV and radio stations. If they don't want the world to know what they've done, the news will never get out."

"In that case, I agree with Eric," Grace said. "It's up to us."

Pasadena Sun

August 13, 2026

GLOBAL-1 SCOFFS AT TRIBAL COUNCIL WARNING. LOUDON WATERS CALLS IT FEARMONGERING OF THE LOWEST ORDER.

President Loudon Waters has publicly dismissed the warnings of the Tribal Council held recently in Canyon de Chelly, Arizona, as "bunk." The council, which comprises representatives from all the Native American

Nations, has flooded the media with claims of an "end of days" scenario claiming that some obscure prophecy dating back to earliest civilization has finally come to pass.

"If these people feel the need to call attention to themselves and their various complaints, let them do it without trying to arouse mass hysteria," the president went on to say. "Global-1's team of the most eminent scientists in the world assure me that the meteor is safely traveling its path and there is no need whatsoever to be concerned that it, or anything else, threatens our way of life."

Global-1 has banned all its stations and affiliates from carrying news of the Tribal Council's warnings. The Cherokee medicine woman known only as Eutonah, recently released from the female Bedford Hills Correctional Facility where she had been imprisoned for her role in bar code tattoo resistance, told a local TV station, "The people of the world must take our warnings seriously," before static engulfed her message. The station's broadcast license was consequently revoked.

"My advice is to carry on with your lives and don't worry," said President Waters. "I'm told that in twelve days when the meteor passes by us we'll get a terrific light display in the sky. My family and I will be out on the White House lawn to see it. You can rest assured of that."

TWENTY

"What do we do now?" Kayla asked. The Decode group, along with members of the Drakians, were assembled back at the Decode cave headquarters in the Great Basin Desert. There was murmured conversation, but no one offered a plan.

Grace sat beside Eric, Eutonah, and Chief Russell, watching the group. Eutonah rose to speak and everyone grew silent. "We must get the word out. That is our most important mission as I see it right now. We must all consider ourselves Postmen and go out to spread the word. Right now we have only each other."

"I agree." Everyone turned to see David Young striding into the cave along with his father, Ambrose Young. "We have to organize shelters worldwide."

"What's going to happen exactly?" Kayla called out.

"We're not sure, but we believe Chief Russell Chaca," Ambrose Young said. "In twelve days something dramatic will occur; something potentially devastating to our planet. Global-1, which controls not only our government but the governments of many nations with its financial dominance, has made it clear that it will not be utilizing any resources to assist. It is up to us."

"Face it! It's the end of the world!" a woman from the crowd shouted, inspiring another wave of anguished murmuring.

David Young held his arms up to quiet the crowd. "If it is, in fact, the end of the world, let us go out helping one another."

"How do you want us to start doing that?" Mfumbe asked as he climbed onto a flat rock. "Should we organize into task groups?"

David Young agreed that Mfumbe should divide them into groups, some to create leaflets on handmade presses, others to solicit donations for supplies. Anyone with medical expertise was to form a group, and Postmen would set off chains of oral communications that would hopefully spread like wildfire among communities and eventually travel worldwide. A squadron of hackers would also work at breaking Global-1's hold on the media.

When David Young noticed Grace standing there, he smiled at her. "What happens if this doesn't work?" she asked him.

"At least we'll all be too busy to worry," the Decode leader said with a smile. "I'd rather go out trying than sitting around shivering with fear."

That made sense to Grace, scared as she was. Eric put his arm around her. "If this is the end, then we'll meet it together, Grace," he said.

Letting herself melt into his arms, Grace raised her face as he kissed her. She held him tightly and his warmth melted — at least for the moment — the icy shards of fear forming inside her.

The group fell asleep late that night, sprawling anywhere they could find a spot to throw down blankets or a sleeping bag. Grace slept deeply, exhausted from her return ride from Arizona on the back of the motorcycle and all the events that had come before.

She dreamed of the dances and chants she'd witnessed at the Tribal Council they'd attended, where Eutonah and Chief Russell had presented the other half of the tablet to the assembled shamans and elders. The discovery engendered huge excitement. The elders agreed with Chief Russell's interpretation of the pictograph. Whatever was going to happen, it had to do with technology and it would happen very soon.

The red clay tones of the earth against the vivid yellow of the sky colored Grace's dreams. The impassioned songs of the tribal elders still played in her sleeping mind. Waking, she remembered how the tribes had called upon the Great Spirit to drive Global-1 from their lands since it was Global-1 that was pulling the precious mineral ore and underground waters from the sacred lands.

Then Grace fell asleep once more and dreamed of a giant, many-colored, fire-breathing bird diving into the ocean at tremendous speed. She awoke with a jolt.

This time she heard the crackle of a burning campfire. Kayla, Mfumbe, Allyson, Katie, Eric, and Jack stood by it, streaked with war paint. Grace sat up, alarmed. What were they doing?

And then she saw for herself. They were painting a mural on the cave walls and they were simply splashed with the paints they'd been using. Kayla saw that Grace was watching and smiled. "If this is the end of the world, we want to leave something behind," she explained. "Maybe someday someone will come back and wonder what happened to us."

"It's like the cave people left their drawings behind for us so many thousands of years ago," Mfumbe added.

They had already made a lot of progress and the mural was nearly fifteen feet long and almost ten feet high. It showed the GlobalHelix building with its spiral DNA roof sculpture. There was a section showing bar-coded wrists on weeping people. An outline of a six-foot human figure had its circulatory system mapped out in red. The molecule-sized nanobots dotted the red lines and sent jagged lines up to satellites drawn in the sky. More lines showed signals being sent back to GlobalHelix.

Eric sat down beside Grace, still holding his paintbrush. "It reminds me of the prophecy tablet," he remarked.

"It does," Grace agreed.

Eric took her hand, and together they went over to the part of the mural that Allyson and Jack were working on. It was a vivid blue sky with a dozen swing-los in the air. "Have you built twelve of them already?" Grace asked.

"Almost," Jack said. "When you have the right equipment, they're not that hard to put together."

"Plus, we have room out here to work and lots of people to help us," Allyson added as she painted in an ocher-colored line on a tabletop mesa just below one of the crafts.

David Young approached them, taking in the mural. "Wonderful," he praised the work. "I heard you say you had twelve made?" he checked with Jack. "How fast can you make more?"

"How much money have you got?" Jack countered.

"A *lot* of money," David Young replied.

"Then I can make a lot of swing-los," Jack confirmed with confidence.

"And is the cloaking device working?" David Young asked.

"Like a dream," Jack assured him.

"Wait a minute. There's something I don't understand," Allyson cut in. "If we're facing imminent disaster, why are you so eager to rush production along? It's sort of an inopportune moment to be going into business, isn't it?"

David Young sighed and a sad smile formed on his lips. "When I decided to fund you guys, I was never really concerned with making money. I already have money."

"Then why did you do it?" Allyson asked.

David Young shrugged. "Maybe it won't be the end of the world. Who knows? Maybe we're all just panicked for nothing."

"But you said you didn't care about the money?" Grace reminded him.

"I'm a strange guy, I guess. I just like to see good ideas succeed. And I'm not one hundred percent sure this is the end. Maybe nothing at all will happen just like nothing has come of any of these end-of-times predictions in the past."

"Oh, something is about to happen, all right," Dr. Harriman said, joining them. He had been spending most of his time on his own, in a makeshift laboratory — but he still wouldn't say what he was doing. "I'm not a superstitious man and I don't believe in prophecy or prediction. The mystical mechanisms of otherworldly communications are beyond my understanding. But I am in communication with a vast network of scientists who work covertly so as not to have their findings co-opted by Global-1. Among these colleagues are astrologists and astrophysicists."

"What do they tell you?" David Young asked.

"This solar flare activity is unprecedented. It is already disrupting radio signals worldwide. If it gets any more active, it has the potential to knock satellites out of the sky with the intense heat or jam their ability to receive or send signals."

Mfumbe stopped working on his part of the mural. "Does that affect the space stations?"

"It could," Dr. Harriman replied.

"What about the meteor?" Grace asked.

Dr. Harriman's eyes traveled across the group and Grace sensed his reluctance to tell them what he had to say. Everyone felt it and stopped what they were doing to pay attention. "If any of those disabled space stations get in the path of the meteor, they could dramatically shift its trajectory."

"And send it toward Earth?" Mfumbe asked.

"And send it toward Earth," Dr. Harriman echoed somberly.

Grace's breath caught in her chest. She knew that a meteor hit was what had wiped out the dinosaurs. Was it possible that these were really their last days on Earth? Closing her eyes, she felt the ground beneath her spin and she staggered, feeling faint.

Eric caught her arm. "Steady," he urged softly.

Breathing deeply, Grace willed herself to be strong. "I'm all right," she told Eric as she bent forward to bring blood circulation back into her head. As she hung there, hot tears brimmed her eyes and she realized how much she loved being alive. The idea that very soon she might no longer live — that none of them would — was more than she could cope with.

The Bar Code Prophecy had to be wrong. It *had* to be.

But a line from the prophecy played and re-played in her mind. *The heavenly bodies will be pulled from the skies.* Was that what Global-1 had done? By taking the precious resources from the Earth, had they upset the balance of the universe so that this meteor would be pulled from the skies?

It certainly fit.

Grace wanted her family, but they weren't here. Instead, she looked around at this strange new family she'd found.

And she thought, *What are we going to do?*

TWENTY-ONE

"Why isn't this all over the news?" Kayla fretted several days later as she, Mfumbe, Eric, and Grace stood at the mouth of the cave with several other Decode members looking out. It seemed to Grace that the sky had grown much more yellow and that the heat had become nearly unbearable.

"Even if we don't care about being tracked, we can't get a phone to work," Kayla went on in an agitated tone. "Are we supposed to just wait here for this meteor to blast us to bits?"

Mfumbe put his arm around her shoulders but said nothing. His serious expression radiated the tension they all felt. "Maybe a Postman will come with news," Mfumbe suggested.

"Grace and I are Postmen. I think we should go see what we can find," Eric offered.

Dr. Harriman joined them from inside the cave. "I may have an easier way."

Grace turned along with the others and saw that he held a disc in the palm of his hand. "Grace, this is the invention that has caused you so much trouble," Dr. Harriman revealed. "It's the thing I won't give Global-1, the thing that they want so desperately. I've only now finished it. But I think it might just work."

"What is it?" Grace asked him.

"It's a messaging device that bypasses the satellites," Dr. Harriman replied. "It can be bounced off any metal that's floating in space — any meteor, any planet or asteroid."

"But no one can own those things," Kayla said.

"Oh, the countries and companies are trying, but so far, no. They can't. It's free communication for the planet with no one monitoring it."

"I can see why Global-1 wouldn't want that to get out," Mfumbe remarked.

"It would be far too empowering to humankind," Dr. Harriman concurred. "But we can use it right now to see what's going on out in the world." Sweeping his fingertips across the screen made the device light up. Several taps brought a picture to the screen. "Jonathan! It works!" a man on the screen said. "Good to see you. Is Grace with you?"

"Dad!" Grace cried out, recognizing the voice immediately. "I'm here!" She stood beside Dr. Harriman, looking at her dad, Albert Morrow, on the screen. "Is everyone all right?"

"We're fine, Grace. We were so worried until Jonathan got in touch and told us you were okay," her father replied.

"What do you hear?" Dr. Harriman asked. "We have a news blackout here."

"So do we. Global-1 isn't letting any news through. They're claiming that solar flares have created havoc on all their systems. They probably just want to run for cover before anyone else can."

"Cover from what?" Grace asked.

"The rumors are that the solar flares have knocked out all the controls of the International Space Station and that it drifted and collided with the meteor. Both are headed for Earth's atmosphere as we speak."

"Does anyone know where they might be expected to land?" Dr. Harriman asked.

"Right now they're saying they're going to hit in the Pacific, somewhere near the California/Mexico border."

"How close to land?" Dr. Harriman inquired.

"No one knows."

"How soon?" Dr. Harriman asked.

"They're basing their calculations loosely on Skylab, which fell to Earth in 1979," Albert Morrow explained. "There were nine days between the time the space station hit the atmosphere and when it struck the Earth. But that's just an educated guess. There's a lot more tonnage coming down on us this time."

"Hmm," Dr. Harriman mused. "My colleagues at NORAD estimated the meteor to be twenty million tons and traveling at a speed of twenty-three thousand miles an hour. I have no information on how heavy the current space station is or how much of it will actually hit us. But I can tell you this: Even if some of the space station rips apart and the meteor splits in the atmosphere upon entry, we're still looking at an impact equivalent to many atomic bombs."

The low hum of conversation that had arisen suddenly quieted. Everyone had caught the last statement and was stunned by it. David Young and Ambrose Young had come in, and they appeared as shocked as the rest of them.

"We're looking at nine days?" David Young checked.

"I don't think we have that much time," Dr. Harriman said. "We have two huge objects hurtling toward us. Even if the space station burns up completely and the meteor cracks in half and one whole half fragment . . ."

"Even then?" Ambrose Young questioned.

"I'm afraid so," Dr. Harriman confirmed. "I'm estimating it will reach our atmosphere in another two days and then it will be another two days from the time it reaches our atmosphere to the time it hits us."

Grace's skin went icy with terror and a nausea began to swirl in her belly. This was it then. No one would escape this.

In a mere four days — maybe a day more, maybe a day less — they would all die.

Grace turned toward Dr. Harriman's device as her father's voice came on. "Jonathan. Can I speak to Grace a moment?"

Dr. Harriman handed Grace his device and Grace peered down at her serious-faced father on the screen. "Grace, you know how much we all love you," he began. "I wish we could be together right now. This isn't what we planned."

"I know, Dad," Grace answered as tears welled in her eyes. "I love you, too. I'll be all right. I have good friends here." Tearfully, Grace spoke to her mother, James, and Kim.

"Grace," her mother signed off by kissing her fingers and touching them to the screen. Grace did the same as the screen went dark. The idea that she would never see any of them again caused a deep pain in the pit of her stomach. Her mind wouldn't accept it, as much as she knew she should face the facts.

"Okay, everybody," David Young spoke in a no-nonsense tone. "I was just out with Jack and Allyson. Let's get out and tell everyone what we just now heard. Anyone who's brave enough to try a swing-lo, go out there now and get a flying lesson if you need one. Anyone with Postman experience, please go first."

"Why even bother?" Allyson asked in a despairing tone.

"Because there's a chance," David Young answered.

"Is there, Dr. Harriman?" Allyson asked. "Is there any chance at all?"

"There's always a chance things will not happen as predicted. Right now we don't have all the information," Dr. Harriman answered. "The armed forces might be working on something, a way to move the meteor and the space station out into the ocean. They might be firing nukes at it to blow it apart, though I don't want to think about the kind of nuclear winter that will cause. All these factors make the outcome uncertain."

"So there's a chance we might survive," Kayla surmised.

"There's always a chance," Dr. Harriman repeated.

"I say let's get out to the swing-los," Jack said. "We might as well go out fighting."

A murmur of agreement swept through the group and they began to head toward the front of the cave. Eric came alongside Grace and put his arm around her. "What do you think?" he asked.

"There's no sense just sitting and waiting for the end," she said.

Eric smiled at Grace as she wiped her eyes. "Let's do this together," he suggested. "Hopefully we won't have to parachute out this time."

"I think I should drive on my own," Grace countered. "There aren't that many people who've even been in one before. At least I have that much experience." Grace wasn't sure she could do it and was frightened, but another part of her was thrilled at the idea of trying.

Grace adjusted the brim of her cap so that it sat above her dark sunglasses. The soaked washcloth she'd wrapped around her neck was drying quickly in the blistering sun, and she hoped she'd have a chance to wet it again before flying her swing-lo across the desert.

Seeing her family again had made her long to be with them. But hearing their tender words had lifted a weight from her heart. At least she knew where they were and they had said their good-byes, if that's what it would come to.

The swing-los were parked in a line of twelve outside a wooden lean-to Allyson and Jack had been using as a workshop. With the sun reflecting off their sides, the crafts appeared sleeker and more state-of-the art than ever before.

Katie's tractor trailer was parked nearby. She stood in back with the doors open. Behind her were stacks of boxes filled with emergency supplies: water, food, first-aid kits.

"Ordinarily each swing-lo can carry two people, but today we're using only one pilot to each vehicle so that you can load the passenger seat with these supplies," Allyson told the group of pilots that she and Jack had selected and given a quick training session. Grace joined the others in loading her craft with the boxes.

"Do we have cloaking technology on these now?" Eric asked.

"It's installed but because of these solar flares I can't get it to work," Jack replied.

Grace's swing-lo was parked beside the one Eric intended to fly. "Do you think what we're doing will make any difference?" Grace asked skeptically.

Eric continued to stack his boxes as he spoke. "The space station will break up when it hits the atmosphere and will probably crash all around us in pieces. And, like Dr. Harriman said, the meteor might split apart, but still . . . when that hits . . ." He let his voice trail off ominously.

Grace shut her eyes and let her mind go blank. She didn't want to envision — even in her imagination — the disasters his unspoken words implied. If the meteor hit the Pacific, then a large part of the ocean was going to end up crashing into the coasts. And that was the best-case scenario. Maybe the tidal wave would be contained by the various mountain ranges in its path but it would all depend on the force and size of the tsunami.

"Do you think the armed forces will come out? Can the navy do anything?" Grace asked.

"Who knows?" Eric answered, coming around beside her. He held her in his arms and she laid her head on his chest. His heart pounded and he tightened his grip in a way she found reassuring. "Grace, I'm glad we're going to be together, whatever happens. You've come to mean so much to me."

Grace looked up at him. "I feel the same."

He smiled at her and brushed away a piece of hair that had fallen into her face. "I love you, Grace."

His words brought emotional tears to her eyes, a mix of happiness and something else. She couldn't name the something else. Maybe it was being overwhelmed by feelings — to have found something so precious as his love and to know that there would be no real time for them to be together — it was so confusing.

"I love you, too, Eric," Grace said, knowing it was so. They leaned toward each other and kissed. For a moment, the world went away. There was no Global-1, no prophecy, no tidal wave crashing toward them. For a moment Grace let herself imagine that this was happening in her backyard as she had hoped it would not so very long ago.

When the kiss was done, they slowly parted, still looking at each other. "We'd better get going," Eric said, finally. "Are you going to be all right flying that thing?"

"Of course," Grace replied, wishing that the confidence in her tone was sincere and not the false bravado that it really was. She hoped she could remember Jack's quick instructions, which, at the moment, she recalled as only a blur of words.

Pushing these worries aside, Grace climbed into the pilot's seat of the cockpit. The new, improved swing-lo had a stream-lined dashboard that rose with three-dimensional holographic controls when she waved her hand across its rectangular screen. Its steering mechanism was gone, replaced with finger-touch technology. Its engine purred to life when she activated the controls as Jack had showed her, and the craft elevated smoothly to about three feet above the ground.

Grace stole a glance at Eric, who hovered beside her. He smiled and shot her a thumbs-up. "Final level, huh!" he remarked.

Grinning, she nodded.

"All right, everyone," Allyson spoke loudly to the group. "Remember not to take these too high. The last model cracked up at a thousand feet. We're pretty sure they can now climb to about thirteen hundred feet, but we're not positive. At no higher than eight hundred feet, any of these buttes and mesas should be possible landing platforms if you don't want to come all the way down. Good luck and remember to meet us at Monument Valley by the formation called The Thumb when you're done. We're going to meet with the tribal elders there. At least we'll all see this through together."

Grace slid her finger up the side of the orange holographic bar and the craft rose ten feet in the air. Immediately her swing-lo tilted so far to the right that Grace gripped its sides. The auto-correct kicked in, placing her back into a horizontal equilibrium.

"Don't worry, you're doing better than most," Eric said as he hovered at her side. Gazing in the direction he was pointing, she saw that the other ten pilots were having an initial rough start, some spinning in circles, others jerking abruptly up and down, still others lurching forward and back.

Eric whizzed off to help other struggling new pilots while Grace practiced flying at three feet around the desert floor. Before long she felt a new confidence and rose two feet higher and flew faster. Soon she was ready to elevate even higher.

Smiling with the pleasure of near-mastery, Grace maneuvered the swing-lo in a swirling, pretzel-like pattern, dipping around and under in arching curves. Pressing down on the purple bar of the holographic accelerator, she sped out away from the group into the desert, traveling at fifteen feet above the ground. She set the navigator toward Sedona, Arizona. She would stop along the way and offer one of her supply boxes, telling the people what she knew, inviting them to join the others in Monument Valley at The Thumb. The higher ground they could make, the better.

As Grace flew, she was filled with a joyful, almost desperate exhilaration. If these were going to be the last hours of her life, then she could think of no better way of spending them than flying free as a bird on the most exciting adventure of her life.

TWENTY-TWO

For the next three days, Grace worked to perfect her skills as a swing-lo pilot. The training went well; she seemed to have a natural aptitude for it. She didn't think any of the fleet, except Jack, Allyson, and possibly Eric were any better than she was now. It wasn't just her opinion. They all said so.

She was grateful to have the flying to concentrate on. If she'd only been sitting and waiting for the end to come, she was sure she'd have lost her mind to fear and anxiety before the actual event even occurred. But maybe she wouldn't have, she considered. Spending this time with Eric, both knowing it might be the only time they would ever have, made the days sweet in a strange, unexpected way.

Who would have thought that the last days of the world would turn out to be the best days of her life?

Now she was on her way into Monument Valley, flying just above the highway with the bubble-top open. The heat had become so intense that no one could bear to close the clear dome over themselves. As the yellow sky began to fade back into dusk, Grace touched the tip of her nose and cringed with pain. Despite the coverage of her cap and a liberal smear of sun block, it was badly sunburned.

Hours spent flying across the desert, stopping only to talk with people in Sedona and then the village of Chinle had left her skin burned and her muscles aching but her mood uplifted. She felt useful, and knowing that Global-1 couldn't track her because of their signal jams made her feel free for the first time in weeks. She hadn't realized how much having the tracker nanobots in her bloodstream had depressed her, made her feel like a trapped animal.

On her way into Monument Valley, she saw Global-1 mining trucks rumbling along the highway, their cloaking devices no longer functional. It seemed strange that they were working despite everything that was happening in the world.

Her monitor indicated that another swing-lo was behind her. In a little while she saw it was Eric who was piloting it. Slowing so he could come alongside her, she saw that his expression was serious.

"It's happened, Grace!" He shouted to be heard over the wind and engine noise. "The meteor has hit the Pacific Ocean at San Diego. A thousand-foot tsunami is traveling at two hundred miles an hour and is headed our way."

One by one the twelve swing-los appeared in the valley, hovering alongside one another. "We have to bring as many people as we can up to the ridges and mesas," Eric told the others.

The group flew to The Thumb, where the Tribal Council was gathered. The members of Decode and the Drakians had joined the tribal elders there. The pilots loaded them two at a time into their swing-los, which shimmied with the added weight of an extra load.

"Take Chief Russell," Eutonah said when Grace stopped for her. "I'll stay down here to help load." As the elderly chief climbed in, Grace saw that Kayla, Mfumbe, Allyson, and Jack were helping guide people into the crafts. David Young and his father were also lending a hand.

Dr. Harriman approached Grace, gripping his handheld invention. "This device is still working," he told her. "I've been able to alert government officials in Denver, Salt Lake City, and Spokane."

"Get in," Grace urged him. "Maybe it will be easier the higher you go."

The swing-lo tipped as Dr. Harriman climbed aboard, squeezing next to Chief Russell. It shimmied ominously but then adjusted and began to slowly ascend. The shaking grew increasingly violent as they neared the top of West Mitten Butte. Grace's gauge read 5,597 feet above sea level. This was higher than she should be going. But the other swing-los were managing it, though also shaking badly.

For hours, Grace and her companions worked to bring the Tribal Council, Decode workers, and Drakians up. The last yellow of the sky was fading into darkness as the pilots hovered in a group, scanning the canyon floor, searching for anyone they might have missed.

Above the hum of the crafts, Grace slowly detected an unfamiliar sound. A low roar was approaching from somewhere. The others heard it, stretching up high in their crafts to hear better.

Grace caught Eric's eye and he nodded, telling her he was thinking the same thing she was: It was here.

Below, water glistened, reflecting the full moon as it seeped into the valley.

Global-1 trucks began to rumble down Highway 163 as workers realized what was happening and tried to flee.

Grace's swing-lo began to vibrate until the shaking traveled into her body, making her bones buzz with the sensation, her teeth chatter uncontrollably.

The rumbling roar grew into a deafening blast.

And then it appeared. A thousand foot wall of water rolled in from the west.

On the ground, Global-1 workers had climbed onto their trucks and machinery. Waving their arms at the swing-los, they shouted to be rescued.

Without thinking, Grace swooped down and took on two men. The others were immediately behind her, picking up as many of the stranded workers as they could manage.

A seam of Grace's craft vibrated loose, pulling apart in an ever widening gap as she went down a second time for another couple of workers. *No, no!* she thought desperately. *Hold on just a little longer,* she coaxed the craft as though it were a living being she could urge on.

As she traveled back up with another group, Grace was pelted with water. In a minute the tidal wave would engulf them. Depositing the workers on the mesa, Grace saw that Eric had zoomed down to get two more.

Was he crazy? There was no time to bring them back up!

His ship was wobbling horribly.

The two passengers were thrown free of the craft. In the

next second, Eric's swing-lo flew apart, its pieces flying in every direction.

At the same moment, the gigantic wave hit, tossing him into the air, arms and legs sprawled.

"No!" Grace shouted as she watched from above.

Setting the controls into a steep dive, she flew down. By the time she neared him, Eric was in the water, struggling to keep his head above but being driven under by the force of the surge. As Grace came above the driving wave, her craft was tossed away as though it were no more than a feather.

It was no use. She would never reach him.

The gap in her swing-lo was widening. If it pulled completely apart, the craft would be destroyed just as Eric's swing-lo had been.

The parachutes! Every swing-lo had one. But that couldn't help them now.

Grace reached under her seat for her chute as a new idea came to her. Unfurling it, she let the parachute and its lines drop. Coming as low as she could manage, she dragged the chute to Eric, who floundered in the water.

He grabbed and missed repeatedly. It was just too far up.

Desperate to reach him, Grace threw her weight onto the side of swing-lo, tipping it to such a steep pitch that she had to grip the side to keep from being thrown overboard.

The nylon chute skimmed the top of the wave and Eric caught it. Pulling herself back into the cockpit, Grace ran her fingers up the holographic bar and the craft lifted.

Tremendous winds generated by the tsunami swirled

around them, keeping Grace's swing-lo from climbing, blowing it sideways instead.

The gap widened and Grace clutched at it with both hands, struggling to keep the craft together by the desperate strength in her arms. A gust caught the ship from the side and pitched it into the side of the butte, smashing it against the rock wall.

The lines of the parachute snagged against a rock ledge as Grace tumbled into the chute.

Hanging there breathless, just above the level of the rising flood, Grace saw that the lines Eric had clung to were now underwater.

"Eric!" she shouted down.

Seeing no sign of him, she searched the racing flood waters. Had he been thrown loose? Swept away?

In the next minute, Eric emerged, climbing up the battered parachute.

Grace had never seen a more wonderful sight.

Hoping that the parachute would not come loose from the rock wall, Grace also pulled herself arm over aching arm, the wet nylon slipping and cutting into her skin, until she was able to pull herself onto the ledge. Eric was quickly beside her.

Peering upward, they saw the people on the rock, looking down. They were safely above the water.

Eric enfolded Grace in his arms, and she clung to him, both of them exhausted from the effort of climbing, huddled there on the rocky ledge.

■ ■ ■

Grace opened her eyes to see that the red and pink sky was streaked with vivid blue as the sun rose. The garish yellow of the last days had faded back to a lemony glow. She had fallen asleep in Eric's arms, both of their backs propped against a boulder. He still slumbered beside her. They were both bruised and disheveled, but alive. She remembered everything that had happened, including being transported to the mesa top by Jack who came to get them in a swing-lo.

Leaning forward, Grace was amazed to see that the violent energy of the tsunami had subsided into rolling waves that crashed just below the top of the mesa. The space was crowded with people. Looking across to East Mitten Butte, she saw that many people were crowded onto its top, as well.

Kayla came and sat beside Grace. "How are you feeling?"

"Banged up. Okay," Grace responded.

"Dr. Harriman has been on his device. He's spoken with your family. They're okay even though there's huge flooding on the East Coast, too. Global-1's space station and satellites all fell in the Gulf of Mexico. The Chinese space station went into the Pacific in Asia. Other space stations and satellites also went down. The entire world is pretty much underwater."

"The whole world?" Grace questioned, aghast at the immensity of the disaster.

"Not entirely. A lot of people got to the mountains. People in higher elevations probably did better than those closer to sea level. We don't have all the information yet. The good news is that Global-1 headquarters worldwide have been destroyed and all its satellites and space stations are down."

Blinking to consciousness, Eric awoke and surveyed the

changed scenery around him. "I don't believe it," he murmured as a wave rolled in just yards away.

Mfumbe joined them and looked out over the water. "Your premonition has come true, Kayla," he said. "The desert has turned back into an ocean."

Mfumbe folded his arms and leaned against the boulder. "You know, when I was a kid I was taught in Bible class that the world would never again be destroyed by flood like it was back in Noah's ark times."

Kayla rose and took his hand. "It's not destroyed."

"It's just been given a second chance," said Eutonah, joining them.

They stood silently for several more minutes, taking it all in before walking off. While Eric spoke with his mother and uncle, Grace wandered around the mesa, seeing what was happening. People were already engaged in the business of survival: making fires, tending to the injured, setting up shelters. A crowd gathered around Dr. Harriman, trying to get news of what had happened. Jack and Allyson guided a team in repairing the battered swing-lo fleet.

In a while, Grace would help, but she just needed a little time to think about everything that had happened. No doubt, a lot of people had died and she took a moment to mourn them.

Eric came up alongside her and took her hand. "My mother has had one of her visions," he told Grace. "She doesn't think Global-1 is coming back. They've suffered too much damage."

Grace let a warm breeze waft over her. "So nobody is receiving signals from the nanobots in my blood anymore?" she questioned.

"There are no satellites to pick up your signals. If they're not active, Dr. Harriman told me they'll dissolve in six months," Eric said.

Shutting her eyes, Grace absorbed this information. She allowed the low flame of relief and happiness to catch fire within her. The net that had been thrown over all of them had been torn loose.

"Do you think this is really a second chance for the world?" Grace asked Eric.

"It could be," he allowed. "I hope it is."

In her heart, Grace was certain it was a second chance. "And this time maybe, we can do it right," she said. "We can sure try."